Where was she?

Disjointed images of bears and yellow-eyed monsters flashed, like lightning, through Michaela's mind.

She looked around, searching for some familiar landmark. Instead, she found the cause of her disquiet. He watched from the shadowy grove of spruce to her left, as if intentionally shielding himself from view. He squatted, staring with intent, predatory eyes.

His thick brown hair hung loose, brushing his wide shoulders. He did not smile. His tanned skin glowed a deep golden hue, a shade darker than hers. She had not met him, for she certainly would have remembered such a man.

He seemed invincible. Powerful enough to frighten off the ghostly eyed black bear without drawing a weapon. Yes, she recalled him now, standing fearlessly before the vaporous thing that stalked her.

Every part of him was larger than life, from his fierce expression to his powerful restraint. He stood completely still, radiating danger.

He stepped from the shadows, revealing himself, and her sense of vulnerability grew.

Books by Jenna Kernan

Silhouette Nocturne

Dream Stalker #78

JENNA KERNAN

writes fast-paced romantic adventures, set in out-of-the-way places and populated with larger-than-life characters.

Happily married to her college sweetheart, Jenna shares a love of the outdoors with her husband. The couple enjoys treasure hunting all over the country, searching for natural gold nuggets and precious and semiprecious stones.

Jenna has been nominated for two RITA® Awards and is a popular speaker at writing conferences. Visit Jenna at her Internet home, www.jennakernan.com.

DREAM STALKER

JENNA KERNAN

Silhouette® Books

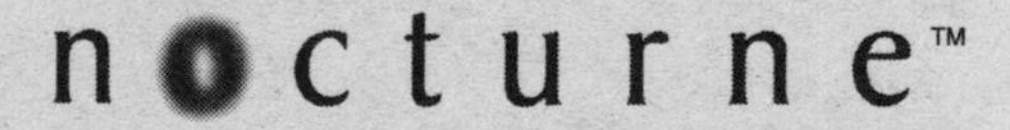

Recycling programs for this product may not exist in your area.

ISBN-13: 978-0-373-61825-5

DREAM STALKER

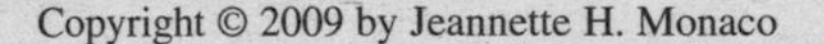

This edition published by arrangement with Harlequin Books S.A.

www.silhouettenocturne.com

Printed in U.S.A.

Dear Reader,

I first came upon the word *skinwalker* while reading a novel by Tony Hillerman and was intrigued by these Native American shape-shifters, who, unlike the werewolves of Eastern Europe, have the advantage of being homegrown. Although Lakota myths may not be familiar to all readers, they are no less fascinating.

In this story, you will meet Michaela Proud, a woman who discovers her nightmares are real. She is being stalked by the god of death and only a shape-shifting grizzly can save her. Her rescuer has pitted himself against the ruler of all ghosts, who knows the woman is more than human.

I hope you love Sebastian and Michaela as much as I do and that you are thoroughly entertained by their weird and unfamiliar world. It has been my great joy to bring these lovers to life and see that their love is tested in the harshest crucible of all, the world of the supernatural.

Please come visit me at my Web home, www.jennakernan.com.

Jenna Kernan

This book is dedicated to the men and women who study, protect and preserve wildlife and wild places.

Chapter 1

Wilmore Wilderness Park, Alberta, Canada

Michaela Proud succeeded in screaming herself awake from her nightmare. She lay in the predawn gloom, bathed in sweat and trembling. The clock beside her on the nightstand ticked like a tiny heartbeat—5:00 a.m.

She was not brave enough to close her eyes again so she swept back the covers and pressed her feet to the cold reality of the drafty floor, safe for the moment.

Michaela rose from her narrow single bed, her ears buzzing with fatigue, and slid into her jeans and a pink lace camisole, before heading downstairs. In the kitchen she flicked on the single overhead light and gripped the worn Formica counter before the sink, leaning forward to stare at her reflection in the dark window beyond. The tiny purple scar at her hairline seemed a trifle. It was hard to believe this was the only visible reminder of the accident that had nearly killed her. The doctors said she was lucky. Michaela saw the beads of sweat on her brow. She didn't feel lucky.

Michaela traced the irregular mark with the tip of her index finger, holding it somehow responsible for her situation. She had never had such dreams before the crash. Now they grew worse each night until she feared she was losing her mind. The doctors prescribed pills, but she'd stopped taking them because under their influence she could not wake and escape the terrible shadow-thing that stalked her dreams.

Something moved behind her. She shifted her eyes, recognizing the spectral figure from her dream. A centipede of terror wiggled up her neck as her heart exploded into wild pounding.

The rasping rattle of breath sounded in her ears, the words barely audible.

"I see you."

She spun.

There was nothing before her but the empty kitchen illuminated by the harsh overhead light she'd turned on.

She exhaled in relief and embarrassment, sagging back against the counter. For just a moment she had feared she was dreaming or that the creature had crossed to her waking reality. That thought brought her spinning back to look in the glass.

Nothing.

"Get a grip," she muttered.

The tapping on the window caused her to cry out as she staggered back. The rhythmic tap came again. Recognizing the sound now, she pressed a hand on her chest in a vain effort to slow her racing heart and, with the other hand, flipped off the light. The world beyond her window appeared, revealing the little chickadee her mother had dubbed Cheeky, for his audacity. There he stood on the windowsill, cocking his head from side to side as he hopped. Cheeky was the feeder-alert system, notifying her mother when it ran empty.

Michaela laughed in relief.

"All right, my friend, message delivered."

She tugged on her boots, knotting the laces, slipped into the long-sleeved denim shirt hanging by the door, and then gathered a canister of sunflower seeds before heading out. She grabbed the footstool as she passed through the shed and marched across the empty yard toward the bird feeder.

The mist swallowed her feet. She inhaled the cool air, feeling suddenly calmer here under the gray sky. Her hand still trembled as she crossed the misty yard, but her heart returned to a steady rhythm.

If only there was some way to fight it. But how does one battle a thing that exists only in the shadows of the mind?

Was this the hallucination Dr. Kent had warned about? The possibility worried her, but what sent an icy shiver down her spine was the chance that the thing was *not* a hallucination. Her gaze darted around the yard.

The mist made the familiar trees seem sinister. Was it here? The silence impelled her to hurry toward the squirrel-proof contraption listing slightly to the left. The box stood just before the line of spruce that marked the forest's edge. Her mom would never have let it stand there empty like that.

Bits of wet grass stuck to her hiking boots as she completed the journey, carefully set the ladder before the metal pole and climbed up to pour the seed. When she finished, she recapped the feeder.

Before turning back, she recalled a little blueberry patch by the stream, just beyond the line of spruce. A handful would be so delicious in her pancakes.

She left the bag of seed and the stepladder before striding off. The long grass quickly soaked her pant legs as she made her way through the trees, finding the low berry bushes with little difficulty. She paused to look around. Only a few steps from the cabin, but already her new home had disappeared, swallowed up by the greenery and mist. She'd come four months ago to recover and stayed after her mother's death. She felt closer to her here, in this place she loved best. Michaela stooped to collect the firm blueberries still wet with dew, choosing only the ones that released easily from their stems.

Unable to shake the feeling of being watched, Michaela reached for her mother's fetish necklace, pulling it out from its hiding place against her skin. She clutched the carved turquoise bear, embellished with a bit of white feather. Her mother had never taken it off, and now it had passed to Michaela. It was Zuni, not Lakota, but her mother said the Zuni made better carvers, and she was of the Bear Clan so it pleased her to wear it. Bears had healing power, according to her mom, though they hadn't prevented the cancer. She wished that bears also protected dreams, for if ever Michaela needed this sort of protection, it was now.

The first and only warning she received was a huffing sound to her right.

Michaela turned to see a large black bear rise to its hind legs only ten feet from where she stooped. Her scream died in her throat, trapped by the squeezing fingers of terror that now seized her.

The bear huffed again and then sniffed the air, causing the slits at the sides of its nostrils to open and close.

What had her mother said about bears? Maggie had been a Tribal Woman, all wisdom and knowledge, while Michaela's experience with nature usually involved the Discovery Channel and a bag of Oreos.

She scrambled for some useful scrap of advice as her heart pounded like a fist in her chest. *Don't get between them and their babies. But there were no babies here. Carry a gun. Too late for that. What else? Don't run—it triggers the chase response. Stand tall. Back away. Make noise.*

Michaela dropped the berries and threw her arms up, shouting, "Ya! Ya! Get away, bear!"

That was when she noticed the gleaming yellow eyes—strange, unnatural, familiar eyes that glowed as if lit from within. Recognition rang inside her like a bell, bringing every nerve ending alive with terror.

She stumbled back and scrambled to regain her footing. The bear dropped to all fours and charged.

Michaela screamed as the bear fell upon her, carrying

her backward into the tall weeds. It lunged for her throat, but she dodged and its terrible fangs sank into her shoulder. She screamed again, this time in agony, as her attacker reared back, lifting a claw to slash at her. With the weight of the bear momentarily removed from her, Michaela rolled to her stomach, curling to protect herself.

My God, it will kill me.

She clasped hold of the bear amulet and prayed.

Sebastian, son of the Great Spirit Bear, Tob Tob, heard the other bear attack but did not interfere. It was the natural order that predators attack the weak, and this human female was weak, indeed. He sniffed the air, sensed the difference and paused. Even wolverines didn't exude such a stench. There was something unnatural here.

He stood in confusion, sniffing the putrid odor of malice that clung to the attacking bear. Once close enough to see the creature and to note the glowing yellow eyes, his hackles rose. Nagi, the Ruler of all Ghosts, was breaking the laws of nature by taking possession of an animal.

Sebastian prepared to strike.

The ghost was strong, a true Superior Spirit, while Sebastian was only a Halfling, the offspring of a Spirit father and a human mother. He doubted he could succeed against Nagi. But it was his place to fight.

The warning growl that issued from Sebastian was deep and low, but the ghost was too distracted by the kill to take note. It was a mistake that Sebastian would make sure he regretted.

He reared up and roared.

Now the ghost-bear recognized him for what he was—an Inanoka, a shape-shifter who could change from animal to human at will.

What little was left of the black bear tried to cower, but Nagi disregarded the danger and forced him forward. *Of course you are not afraid. You can't die. But you are in animal form now, so I can make you suffer.*

Sebastian could not best Nagi, but he could best this little bear. Without his host, Nagi had no body with which to fight. The small male had no chance against a fifteen-hundred-pound grizzly.

Sebastian meant to force the specter out of this animal and back into the shadowy place where it belonged. But how to do it without killing the host?

Nagi charged, and Sebastian met his attack with one swipe of his paw, sending his opponent reeling. Again the bear rushed forward and Sebastian clouted him in the head. The creature staggered and swayed for a moment. On the third charge the bears entwined. Sebastian bit into his opponent's neck, feeling the skin give way as his long incisors sliced through muscle on their way to the spine. Just before he broke its neck, the ghost leaped. Sebastian felt the surge of energy and smelled singed fur. His opponent went limp. Sebastian halted and, hearing a submissive whine, released his jaws.

The black bear fell limp to the ground. Where was Nagi?

He turned to find the specter hovering over the woman, who lay half cloaked in mist. Sebastian eyed the thing that most resembled a living shadow, gray as smoke from a forest fire with putrid yellow eyes that reminded him of an infected wound.

Nagi swooped at him. Sebastian braced as Nagi tried to take possession of his body. He succeeded only in penetrating his skin. Instantly, a scalding pain ignited within him, burning his flesh. He roared in agony and writhed upon the grass, clawing at his own hide as smoke rose from his coat. As suddenly as it began, the pain ceased.

Nagi leaped away, leaving the stench of death clinging to Sebastian's hide. The ghost's vaporous body vibrated; smoke billowed from it in all directions.

Sebastian smiled, knowing the ghost had felt every bit of the pain it had caused him. Apparently, it was too much for the great Nagi.

Sebastian transformed into a man in order to speak. Around his shoulders, he wore his golden brown pelt, now like a cape, fastened at his neck by a single bear claw set in turquoise and silver. The hide never left him, though he often changed its appearance, for without it he would remain in human form.

"How dare you come here?" he roared, his voice gravelly from disuse. He had not been a man in many, many years.

"You have no part in this," hissed the yellow-eyed demon. His voice sounded like water thrown on hot rocks. "Leave her."

Leave her? Sebastian glanced at the male bear in confusion and then recalled the woman. She lay beneath the ethereal Nagi, at the foot of a white birch, clutching her shoulder with one hand and a leather cord, which hung around her neck, with the other.

Was this who Nagi had come for?

He stared at her. Damn, he had shifted right in front of her. She rocked back and forth, her eyes pinched shut. Perhaps she had not seen.

He looked at her closely for the first time. She was small and weak, like a child. The creature had seen fit to protect only her feet, encasing them in a sturdy pair of hiking boots. The rest of her body, sheathed in thin denim jeans, an open shirt and a lacy top, did nothing to shield her from attack. Nagi had torn through her outer garments as if they were paper. Now she huddled, whimpering in pain. Her suffering angered him. He did not mind killing for food, but to torture the creature, as Nagi had done, that was cruel.

Why did Nagi want the woman?

He scowled at the ghost. "She is alive and so beyond your dominion."

"No," howled the ghost, his voice whistling like a gale wind.

"You must wait until she dies to take her. Let her be now."

Humans were not Sebastian's concern. Their care fell to Niyan and his Halfling offspring. But this phantom had drawn Sebastian's wrath when he had used an animal as his pawn. He lowered his head, wishing he could sink his teeth into the ghost. Instead, he took a swing at Nagi, but, as expected, his hand passed right through.

Nagi swooped toward the woman. She threw up her

hands as if to ward off the specter. But that made no sense. Very few humans could see Spirits, even fewer when awake. The only true Seer he'd ever met had succeeded in cultivating his gift only after years of training. Yet he could swear this woman followed Nagi with her eyes, as it gnashed its long pointed teeth menacingly before her. How was that possible?

Nagi raged on. Without the benefit of a physical body, he could do no more than storm. But the woman obviously did not know this, for she cowered against the tree, lifting a forearm across her eyes.

"Be gone now," Sebastian warned. "Even you cannot violate the laws of nature."

The Spirit howled once more, a high keening cry that made Sebastian's skin crawl. Then he turned on Sebastian and glared.

"I go, for I have already won."

Slowly the phantom dissolved into the mist that clung to the brook, leaving Sebastian puzzling over his words. Bravado, he decided, and turned to the injured bear.

He lay where he had fallen; his head limp upon the ground. The torn skin and the raw, bloody muscle showed a grievous injury, but Sebastian had not had to sever the long cords beside the spine. He regretted that this innocent would live with the scars of this terrible day, but at least he would live. Sebastian knelt and placed his hands upon the wounds, sending healing energy deep into the shredded muscle.

"Mend, my brother, and return to your path."

The bear lifted his head with great care.

Sebastian smiled. "It is sore, I know. But you will climb the honey tree before the new moon rises."

The bear cried and then lurched to his feet. He seemed in a hurry to go and Sebastian could not blame him.

Why had the ghost left the bear before Sebastian had killed it? He had witnessed possessions before. A ghost only abandoned a body when forced to do so by a powerful healer or by death. But this was no ordinary ghost—it was the ruler of all. So why had the Spirit been unable to possess him? Was it even possible for a Superior Spirit to possess an Inanoka? Sebastian puzzled over this until he heard a whimper, like a wolf pup crying for its mother. He faced the woman. What about her had drawn the notice of the great Nagi?

Chapter 2

The woman cradled her arm as if it was broken, Sebastian noticed. A mane of thick black hair fell over her face and narrow shoulder, veiling the wound from him.

She lifted her chin, sending her black hair cascading back like a waterfall of silken threads. Her face was wet with sweat and tears. Still, it was a striking face, with dark lashes that fanned high cheekbones. Her wide, curved mouth was open and she panted with labored breath. Her cinnamon skin and angular features told him she was a member of the first people. Did she know the old ways?

She still clenched a necklace in her injured hand, her grip so tight that her knuckles grew white. A cross or star, likely, he thought as he inched closer, suddenly curious.

His instincts told him to be wary of this one for Nagi wanted her, and he only pursued evil souls. Outwardly, she looked like any innocent creature attacked in the circle of life. But humans were masters of deception.

He sniffed, using the keen senses that never left him, even when he took human form. He smelled blueberries first and then the tang of fear and acrid scent of pain and something else, something new. How badly was she injured?

He crept closer still, telling himself with each step that she was none of his concern. But he was curious, always curious. She did not look like most human females he had seen. She was better constructed—lovely, even—in her pain. He paused and squatted before her, and she lifted her gaze to meet his.

He drew a breath as she focused her strange green eyes upon him. They were as radiant as a birch leaf shimmering in the sunlight. Her dark sooty lashes fanned her cheeks as she blinked up at him. She seemed stunned speechless from the attack. Her whining ceased at his approach, but tears continued to course down her pale face. They trickled over her jaw and down the long column of her neck. Sebastian studied the pulse at her throat and noted that it beat too fast.

Still she gripped her necklace. He placed a hand over hers, realizing too late that it was a mistake. She released the pendant and gripped his arm with more strength than he would have thought possible. Her actions sent a shot of animal awareness straight to his core. He stared at her anxious face and then to the amulet swinging against her chest. His eyes widened as he noted the bear effigy.

Sebastian stared at the carved fetish. This was her talisman? Was she one who sought to emulate the powers that were his, one of the Clan of the Bear?

"Why do you wear this?"

"I'm of the Bear Clan," she said.

He didn't know if it was her imploring green eyes or the sight of his likeness around her neck that beckoned. But he answered, wiping the tear tracks from her cheeks.

He glanced toward the tree line that marked the divide between his world and hers. He sniffed the air, but he smelled no one. Cocking his head, he listened for some sound from the old woman who lived in the cabin just beyond the ridge of spruce. Surely this small female did not venture in his wilderness guarded only by this stone pendant?

He should go. The rustling sound brought him around again, but he saw only a whiskey jay hopping through the underbrush. He considered following. The female released his arm.

She made a feeble attempt to draw away the tattered clothing covering her wound. Her pathetic struggle touched him, and he sat beside her. He would wait with her until her people came. In human form, he should not frighten her with his presence, and he could at least protect her from other predators. His gaze narrowed as he wondered if the ghost would have the nerve to return.

Likely he would, but not while Sebastian stood watch. It was unusual for Nagi to leave his realm of shadows, but not unheard-of. But to attack a living being—it was an abomination.

Her panting brought his attention back to her.

"It is gone?" she asked.

He nodded. "For now."

Her eyes widened at this and he realized his qualified answer did not reassure. He could not lie to her. "If it hunts you, it will return in one form or another."

Her brow wrinkled and her gaze no longer seemed focused. Was she dying? That thought brought him to his haunches beside her. If she died, the ghost would have her, and he would be damned if he would let that miserable low-flying cloud be the victor.

He knew what needed to be done, but he dreaded it. He disliked walking among them since a woman as small and weak as this one had shamed him. His cheeks burned at the memory, but he shook it off. She had done him a favor. He preferred the order of nature to the chaos of the world of men. All that woman had done was set him on his true path.

He gazed down at the wounded female, vowing not to be diverted by this one.

He frowned as she glanced around. The sunrise burned away the mist, chasing it back and increasing his line of sight. The lawn before the little cabin was discernible through the spruce. He steeled himself to cross the invisible line. He would carry her that far. Then he would close her wounds, mend her bones and be gone.

"I'll bring you back to your world."

She opened her eyes at this. "My world?"

Sebastian was so accustomed to hauling heavy loads that he was appalled, when he lifted the female, at her frailty and near weightlessness. She stared at him as he carried her, mesmerized him with her bewitching eyes.

Something twitched inside him, some unfamiliar pull, almost as if she, this weak human, posed him some threat. But what could she do to him? The idea was laughable.

He drew her close to his chest and wondered if all females fit so well to their male counterparts. The unfamiliar tug increased and he reconsidered her power. There was definitely something here, for he had picked her up instead of leaving her where he found her and now he did not want to put her down.

"I cannot stay," he said, more to himself than to her.

The sooner he was rid of her, the better. She made him think strange thoughts—rousing, lustful thoughts. He wondered what lay beneath the artificial trappings that humans insisted on wearing and how would she look in the sunlight, robed as Wakan Tanka intended?

The thought caused a rippling excitement that so surprised him, he nearly dropped her. Only then did he recall that humans did not mate in season, but at any time or place. That meant the males were always in rut. No wonder he was having such crazed thoughts.

He walked in the skin of a man and was now subject to all his cravings. He shook his head in disgust, but the action did not serve to clear his mind. It only made him more aware of his tingling skin and the growing urge to stroke this woman.

She placed a hand upon his bare chest. He glared, angry at her for making him wonder what it would feel like to mate with her.

"Do not touch me like that," he cautioned.

Her hand slid away, but the impression still burned.

Sebastian had to stifle the feral growl that rose in his

throat. The female had been through enough without being attacked a second time. It was then that he recalled he wore only a cloak. Was that why they wore the fabric, as a shield from this touch of skin on skin?

He mimicked her clothing. With a single stroke of the claw fastened at his neck, he changed his cloak into a pair of tight blue denim pants and a similar open shirt.

He glanced at her tattered shirt. Where was the blood? Sebastian paused in his stride as he recalled the sight of the bear attacking her. He had gripped her by the shoulder and shaken her as a fox shakes a grouse to break its neck. Why, then, was there no blood?

Something was wrong.

He lowered her to the ground beneath the canopy of green branches. She did not struggle as he propped her against a fallen log and swept back the hair that covered her injuries. His eyes widened with horror as he saw the yellow gleam emanating from the raw, open gash.

"Spirit Wound," he whispered.

From far off came the low rumble of a truck with a hole in its muffler. The rusty pickup appeared on the dirt drive and rumbled slowly up to the cabin. The motor quit. Sebastian crept to the clumps of bright pink fireweed for a closer look.

He spied an older man standing beside the vehicle. The male stared at the bag of birdseed propped beside the folded stepladder; finally he lifted his gaze to the woods beyond. Sebastian ducked.

When he checked again, the man had turned toward the house, calling a greeting, but a moment later he was running down the steps.

"Michaela!"

Sebastian looked at the woman, but she stared straight ahead as if beyond hearing. Had the ghost taken her soul?

No—the body could not survive without that. She was in some trance. He had seen this unnatural stillness in animals caught in the sight of a predator from which there would be no escape. At such times the prey might stand still with eyes wide-open as death took them. But death would not take this little one.

"Where are you?" called the man.

Sebastian froze in indecision. If she had suffered an ordinary wound, he could leave her where the old man would find her. But a Spirit Wound—no human could heal such an injury.

To leave her was to reveal the gap between their worlds, something he had sworn to protect.

Great Mystery, what to do?

Sebastian dragged a hand through his thick hair. He could take her away to die where she would not be found, but if he did, the miserable ghost would have her.

He ground his teeth together, hating his other choice, hating the thought of bringing a human into his world. She would not understand it or him and he would have to remain in human form to treat her, having to suffer these conflicting emotions and crazy ideas. Already she caused him strange sensations whenever they touched. Certainly these longings would only intensify when she roused.

For reasons he did not understand, Nagi pursued this woman. Sebastian knew she had no chance without him. Sebastian crawled back to the woman and gathered her in his arms. Again he felt the savage, gripping urge to protect her. Undoubtedly this was another shortcoming of humans, some innate need to defend the female. He understood instincts and he acted upon them, lifting her into his arms as he crept through the cover of the forest. Traveling fast, he sought the wild places where man could not follow.

Chapter 3

The birdsong reached her, and then a gentle wind brushed her cheek. Michaela blinked her eyes open to find herself propped up against a log in a grassy area. Before her, an unfamiliar stream burbled. The place seemed the picture of serenity. Why, then, were the hairs on her neck rising?

Where was she? Disjointed images of bears and yellow-eyed monsters flashed, like lightning, through her mind.

Michaela's gaze darted about, searching for some familiar landmark. Instead, she found the cause of her disquiet. He watched from the shadowy grove of spruce to her left, as if intentionally shielding himself from view. He squatted on his haunches like a satyr, staring with intent, predatory eyes.

His thick brown hair hung loose, brushing his wide shoulders and further cloaking his features. He did not smile, but rather looked warily at her. His tanned skin glowed a deep golden hue, a shade darker than hers. She had never met him, for she certainly would have remembered such a man. His long nose and slightly angled eyes reminded her of the Lakota, the tribe of her mother. Her tribe, as well, though she had never taken part in tribal politics or ceremony.

He stood slowly, growing with her apprehension. He must be nearly seven feet tall, a giant of a man. He seemed invincible. Powerful enough to frighten off the ghostly eyed black bear without drawing a weapon. Yes, she recalled him now, standing fearlessly before the vaporous specter that stalked her. He had shouted at the monster and it had hissed an unintelligible reply. How was that possible?

Every part of him was larger than life, from his fierce expression to his powerful restraint. He stood completely still, radiating danger as a furnace radiates heat. The intensity of his stare touched off whirlwinds of awareness in her.

He stepped from the shadows, revealing himself, and her sense of vulnerability grew. *Handsome* did not begin to describe his features. Sexy, oh, yes, with a full erotic mouth and square jaw, the perfect complement to his thick dark hair.

She looked up at her savior. This man, this man who was too beautiful to be a man, had rescued her from the yellow-eyed demon. He did not dissolve as the dark shadow had done, but continued forward.

He paused before her, motionless. The menacing air surrounding him made her tremble.

She dropped her gaze, unable to meet the invasion of his stare. It was then that she noticed the necklace he wore. The simple leather cord held an irregular lump of turquoise the size and color of a robin's egg. Fixed beside the stone was a wicked three-inch bear claw encased in sterling silver. The uniqueness of the piece was not lost on her. Most lapidaries polished such valuable stones to more fully reveal the luster. Instead, the maker had chosen not to interfere with the perfection of nature.

The silence stretched and she dared glance at his face once more.

He seemed to be deciding her fate. She sensed his indecision.

"Who are you?" she whispered.

His brow furrowed, and she drew back. "Have you returned to your senses, little rabbit?"

"What happened?"

"What did you *see* happen?"

She closed her eyes and concentrated. Her memory lay broken like shattered pieces of glass. Her doctors had a name for this, something like "psychic break," the separation of the mind from the grim reality of the body. But if she had suffered another brain injury, how could she recall the bear attack in such minute detail? The bear's charge replayed in her mind. She saw it from beyond herself. The beast tore her flesh and shook her like a rag doll. A second bear, the grizzly, charging the first.

She spoke without opening her eyes. "I was attacked."

He squatted at her side, his voice coming soft and commanding. "Yes?"

"There was another bear, a bigger one."

He chuckled, though she could not fathom what was funny. She opened her eyes and found him reaching out. The urge to pull back and the desire to lean forward clashed within her, and so she did nothing at all as he stroked her cheek with his big, callused hand. At his touch, an unexpected sense of calm filled her, as if he had some special power to soothe.

She nearly closed her eyes to savor the contact, but instead she narrowed them on him. Where had he come from?

The deep gravelly quality of his voice made her insides jump as if he stroked her. "What else?" he coaxed.

His hand settled on the juncture of her neck and shoulder.

She closed her eyes to concentrate, thinking back. What she had seen next had no logical explanation.

Her eyes snapped open. "What are you?"

He withdrew his hand. With it went the comfort she had gained from his touch. He clenched his fists, flexing the bulky muscles of his chest. The rock-hard wall of muscle served as a silent reminder of his physical superiority, and she forced herself not to cower as he stood menacingly over her like a raised dagger. She lifted her chin with an air of defiance that did not reach her quaking innards. He stalked away.

Michaela glanced around the unfamiliar surroundings, more afraid of being alone than facing this brooding man. "Don't go."

He paused, his back to her and his posture rigid. Standing there in the forest's dappled light, he looked completely uncivilized. Gradually, he turned until she could see his face in profile.

"You don't know what you ask."

She didn't, but she sensed he understood. She could see it in his troubled eyes, both the wisdom and the power.

"You saw it." Somehow she was certain that he had, and *if* he had, it meant the specter was not some creation of her mind. She clutched at that hope. Her doctors said her problems began and ended in her injured brain. But twice now she had seen the monster while awake—she was awake now, wasn't she? Dr. Kent hadn't believed her. But this man knew otherwise.

He strode back to her like some wild beast, turning her hope to alarm. Her breath caught at the sight of his grace and primal beauty. He stood without presumption and with an aura of supremacy that captivated her. She had never seen a man like him. He crouched beside her with a dangerous confidence that unsettled her. Then he glanced around the deserted clearing, perhaps searching for signs of the nightmare that haunted her. His nostrils flared as he scented the air, as if he could sense things invisible to her.

From this distance, she could see that his deep brown irises were ringed with gold. As she watched, his pupils dilated, adding to her gut impression that he was not what he seemed. He was dangerous, but was he more dangerous than her ghostly attacker?

"Can you protect me from it?"

He did not deny her peril as the doctors had done, nor

did he diminish her fears. Instead, he fixed her with a commanding stare.

"Perhaps."

Michaela's voice grew hushed; she was afraid her nightmare might find her again. "What is it?"

His crouched position and the way he rubbed his cheek with the back of his hand reminded her of a cat cleaning his whiskers, and his golden eyes glowed unnaturally bright. She fought the urge to shrink back.

"You don't belong here." His voice held a distinctive note of resentment as if she had trespassed on his territory.

He grasped a lock of her hair, rubbing it slowly between his thumb and forefinger as if measuring its worth. His hooded, feral expression made her tremble. But she was not sure her reaction stemmed entirely from fear this time. His glance flashed to hers and held. Her breath caught.

He drew away. "I must return you to your people."

Her people, what did that mean—the doctors and psychiatrists? The in-patient facility that they urged her to seek? "They can't help me."

"Of course not."

He glanced at her shoulder. As if triggered by his stare, the searing ache returned, burning into her consciousness and growing like a flame touched to dry tinder.

She gaped at the damage the bear had wrought. The ugly gash began at the top of her shoulder and cut a ragged course down her biceps. The unnatural black edge looked as if she had been burned rather than bitten. Inside the wound, instead of torn muscle and tendon, there emanated an unnatural yellow glow. Panic seized her, and perspiration beaded upon her forehead. She staggered up, making it only as far as her knees.

"What in the world?"

"Not from this world, nor the next, but of the shadowy place between."

The blazing pain now brought suffering with each shallow breath. "Can you help me?"

"Remember that you asked for my aid." He reached, lifting her effortlessly into his arms. "And do not question the manner in which I give it."

She gritted her teeth to keep from screaming at the agony tearing through her, as she huddled in her protector's arms. She prayed for deliverance from the pain as he strode over uneven terrain with fluid grace, coming to a halt on the first patch of level open ground he encountered. There he laid her down.

She clutched at her arm, rolling from side to side and gnashing her teeth to keep from screaming.

He pressed a hand to her shoulder. Even the gentle touch of his fingers made her arm burn. She inhaled sharply and clamped her jaw shut. He closed his eyes. Unnatural heat and a definite feeling of calm permeated her as if he drugged her.

She regarded him with suspicion. "What are you doing?"

"Hush now." He closed his eyes.

"How do you take the pain away?"

One eyelid popped open and he squinted at her. "How do you see Spirits?"

She gaped. "Is that what it is?"

He nodded. His light touch and penetrating calm made

her relax back into the grass. He inspired unwarranted confidence in her and it troubled her more than the pain.

"You see them?" she asked.

"Not often."

"I see them all the time. It used to be just when I slept, but this morning I saw him while awake and then that bear bit me."

"It wasn't his fault. He was possessed."

He said it so matter-of-factly, as if creatures were regularly possessed by Spirits. His words rendered her temporarily speechless.

But now that she thought of it, that did explain the yellow eyes. But not how this man had escaped both bears and the ghost to deliver her quite literally from evil.

"My mother believed in ghosts." She gave him a look, waiting for him to smirk or look away. He did neither. It suddenly seemed important that he understand she did not fall prey to superstitious nonsense. "I don't."

"You know best," he said, removing his hand from her arm.

The pleasant warmth was replaced by a definite chill. Her unease grew. She felt as if she was shuffling farther and farther onto a sheet of very thin ice. But it was all that supported her from the cold, dark nightmares that lay beneath.

She sat up. "You believe in them?"

He nodded. "Of course. But this was not a ghost. It was a Superior Spirit."

The list of Spirits her mother made her learn popped up in her head like the answer to a test question. The Sioux legend was full of Spirits, superior, inferior and even subordinate. She scanned her memory, hardly believing she was even considering this as a possibility as she cradled her injured arm.

She stared at the wound in horror as tendrils of panic choked her. She could not even draw a breath as she studied the iridescent yellow glow pulsing from her open wound. It looked like some movie special effect.

"What is it?" she gasped.

"A Spirit Wound. He has branded your flesh with his mark, like a snake bite, only worse. The poison eats into your flesh until it kills you."

She grabbed her wrist and pulled as if to keep her own arm away from herself. Her gaze flashed from him to the deadly gash. "You have to take me to a doctor."

"No human can heal this."

What did he mean, no human, and what did that make him?

"Can you?"

"I have only succeeded in slowing its progress."

"Then I'll die." She knew it as surely as she knew the earth turned. Another idea came to her, nearly as terrible as death. "Amputate. They could cut off the arm."

"This will not stop it."

"Oh, my God." Tears welled in her eyes and she stared up at him, pleading for help.

"I know of one who may know how to heal this. If anyone can, it is she, for this Supernatural is very powerful. I will take you to her."

She stared at him in horror. Surely she had lost her mind and was trapped in some kind of waking delusion, peopled by all the creatures from her mother's stories.

"This can't be happening."

He said nothing as he stared with eyes that seemed wise and sad all at once.

Michaela glanced again at the unnatural wound, as if to assure herself there was no mistake. But instead of reassurance, the sight of the ugly puss and gore stole her breath way. Her skin went clammy as a buzzing began in her ears.

He touched her. She made an attempt to avoid him, but his hand pressed across her chest, below her collar-bone. Her heart pounded in her ribs, and she felt the heat once more and the sense of calm that came from outside herself, seeping into her being like tea into warm water. Her eyes grew heavy.

She had just enough will to grasp his wrist. "Stop it."

He lifted his brow. "I am only removing your fear."

"It's my fear and I'll keep it, thanks."

He cocked his head again, as if he did not know what to make of her. "Very well."

He drew back his hand until it rested gently on her shoulder. He folded to sit beside her like a yoga instruc-tor meditating on reality.

Left without his magic, she was slammed back to earth like a seesaw that had lost one partner. Either she was mad or she had stepped into a place she did not belong.

"The second."

She stilled as a nasty suspicion formed. "What?"

"A place you do not belong."

Chapter 4

Michaela's eyes widened as her heart galloped once more.

"You can read my mind?"

"A bit."

She looked at his hand resting on the bare skin of her neck just above her collar and slapped it away.

He smiled. "How did you know I must touch you to hear your thoughts?"

How did she?

"What are you, little one?"

She did not know what to say.

He slid an arm beneath her shoulders and knees, lifting her effortlessly into the air.

"Perhaps Kanka will know what to make of you," he said, and turned his face to the sky.

Michaela followed the direction of his gaze, uncertain what to expect, and immediately wished she had not. The sense of surrealism swept her up as her new fractured reality continued to shatter.

Dark swirling clouds swept in and then gathered with unnatural speed. They spiraled ominously, opening at the center to create a dark, gaping mouth. She pointed, stupidly, with her good arm, as if he had not noticed the funnel cloud descending straight at them.

He made no attempt to run. An icy blast leveled the grass in a perfect circle.

Suddenly they began to spin, slowly at first, then faster. Michaela felt them leave the ground and she screamed. But the roaring wind tore away the sound of her voice as they tumbled through space.

She could not breathe, could not see, could not move.

Sebastian felt her struggles but did not relax his grip. To do so was to release her to the Thunderbirds and they did not take kindly to any travelers except the Inanoka.

When her body went slack he grew worried, calling to his friends.

"Take me to my home on the lake, Great Spirits."

Almost instantly he was falling. He knew they were not trying to be rough, but the difference in their size made them clumsy at times. He landed so hard, his knees buckled, but he did not lose his grip. He was almost glad the woman was not conscious, for the jolt would have been agonizing to one with so grievous a wound.

He glanced around and recognized that the Thunderbirds had released him not ten feet from his back deck.

He glanced toward the lake, noting that his Cessna 172 remained safely tied to the dock. The royal-blue-and-white body gleamed in the sunlight, completely untouched by the Whirlwinds. He smiled in admiration at the scalpellike precision of their touchdown.

He made for the log house. It was a luxury to have such a place in an isolated area of the Canadian Rockies, but worth the expense to insure his privacy.

He had hoped to reach the old sorceress, but that journey would do little good if the woman was dead. Even Kanka had her limits. Sebastian gazed down, glad to see the woman's slow, steady breaths.

He took her up the back steps and laid her down at last on a large brown leather sofa. It annoyed him how reluctant he was to release her.

Reaching for the fur blanket on the couch, he tucked it beneath her chin. He stopped himself before he yielded to the impulse to stroke her cheek.

Her skin was softer than the wolf pelt that now brushed her chin. She was a weak and tiny human, yet somehow she had fought the ghost and lived and, according to her own words, not for the first time. He wondered how such a little creature could survive such an onslaught. This human female had a Spirit so formidable that she had staved off the great Nagi himself. Perhaps she was like the wolverine, small but mighty.

He inched closer from his perch on the coffee table, studying her delicate frame. The urge to watch over her only grew as he neared. Her scent rose all about him. Verbena and heather, she smelled like a field of wildflowers. He wanted to roll in her fragrance, bask in that which was only hers. Another odor reached him, putrid and stinking. The ghost wound reeked of death. If he could not heal it, the injury would take her life. As a Spirit bear, he was among the greatest healers but he wondered if even his sire would know what to do with this unnatural wound.

He glanced at her serene face. Her courage called to him, singing a song that only his heart could hear. Such a fearless creature deserved to live. So he would face this battle with her, but first he must fight this invasion.

Michaela blinked open her eyes. She stared up at high cathedral ceilings of warm, blond wood, crisscrossed with massive natural log beams, reinforced with steel joints. Huge smoothly polished rocks formed a massive fireplace that touched the ceiling, dividing the room. Above the mantel hung an oil painting of a grizzly attacking a cowboy. The style reminded her of Remington, one of her favorite artists, but she did not recognize the picture. She stretched, trying to place the unfamiliar. The pain in her arm caused her to stiffen.

The throbbing of her arm made her gasp, and it all came crashing back. She inspected the crisp white gauze bandage circling her upper arm, trying to recall how it got there as she sat up. The action caused the fur blanket to fall to her waist, exposing her naked torso.

It was at that instant that she recalled the man. A strangled sound came from behind her. She glanced over the back of the couch toward the huge bank of windows. There stood the man gripping a dish towel and standing as motionless as if she had stunned him. He stared at her breasts.

A jet flame of mortification fired through her as she grappled with the blanket, shielding herself.

"What are you doing?" she said, her voice sharp with accusation.

He hoisted the dish towel in answer. "You blacked out."

"What did you do with my clothes?"

He pointed to the pile on the coffee table. "Had to dress the wound."

He handed her the wet towel and stepped back as if she might explode.

"Where am I? How did I get here?"

"Don't you recall?" His voice was gravelly, as if from disuse. She found the alluring sound disturbing.

A wild image of clinging to him, as the tornado tried to tear her from his arms, flashed in her mind. Their feet had left the ground. The cold air had seemed devoid of oxygen, and though she'd gasped and choked, it did her no good.

"Ah. I see you are remembering." He lifted a hand and reached for her.

Recalling the peculiar effect of his touch, she scooted away, coming to a stop against the armrest.

The cold apprehension was back, numbing her until her skin tingled. She longed to ask him to take the panic away. She had never felt a coward, but this wound, this man and the unnaturalness of her situation all rose up to make her feel as dizzy as a trauma patient. She pressed the cool cloth to her eyes.

It was too much to absorb. But she would face this, just like she had faced her mother's death, just like she'd faced her nightmares. She refused to fall to pieces.

Michaela drew back the cloth, staring at the man who had somehow moved soundlessly around the couch and now sat on the edge of the coffee table, elbows on knees and hands clasped between his legs. He wore a clean white T-shirt and a pair of jeans that emphasized the musculature of his thighs.

She met his steady gaze. "What was that thing that attacked me?"

"Nagi."

She recognized the name, of course. The Ruler of the Circle of Ghosts, the Spirit who kept watch over evil souls. She narrowed her eyes as she studied her savior for signs he teased her. There were none. No hint, no gesture, just the steady gaze of his intent eyes.

Everything about him relayed his seriousness. Terror ricocheted down her back, straightening her spine.

"Nagi is a legend," she said, babbling her denial more to herself than to him.

She could not think of a more daunting foe. Nagi had touched her. She shivered right down to the center of her being.

Her protector reached out and clasped her hand.

She felt her panic recede like the tide. She was able to think now. The thumping throb of her arm diminished with each beat of her heart. She scowled at him.

"You're doing it again."

"I need to see to your wound."

She slipped her hand free of his, reclaiming her pain. The panic was slower to return, giving her a moment to recall that he had stolen her shirt.

"Give me those."

He exchanged the wet towel for her clothing. She used two fingers to lift the camisole, which was surprisingly free of her blood.

"Turn around."

He scowled, assuring her that he did not take orders often—or at all. She held her breath, recognizing she really did not know who or what she was dealing with. He waited long enough for her to doubt he would do as she bid, and then stood so quickly she gave a little cry. His frown deepened and he turned. In the moment it took to gather her clothing to her, he crossed the room and now stood, one hand lifted to the mantel, motionless, as if he had been waiting there a long time.

She didn't like the uncertainty squeezing her belly.

Michaela slipped the lace top over her head, but pain prevented her from jockeying her injured arm through the ribbon strap.

"I'm stuck."

He turned, assessing her. His touch was gentle as he maneuvered the strap into place.

Without asking, he lifted her denim shirt, frowned at the tattered sleeve and then rent it away as easily as one might tear paper. Then he did the same thing on the other side.

Her fear coiled within her as he held the garment for her for her inspection, smiling benignly as if nothing whatsoever was out of order. His smile faded at her expression.

"It was torn," he said by way of an apology. He wiggled the shirt, holding it open.

She turned to accept his help, stifling a gasp at the pain that came with the motion of lifting her arm.

His strong hands now rested on her bare neck. She dipped her head, allowing the relief, grateful for his comfort.

"I'm taking you outside for the ceremony." With that preamble he scooped her neatly from the sofa, fitting her to his chest and striding away with her.

The momentary indignation at being dictated to dissolved with the sense of power that exuded from this man. His arms were strong, his step sure, and he carried her as if she weighed nothing. For the first time since this madness began she felt safe, because of him. Her mind told her to be wary, but her body believed in him completely.

It's some trick. He's making you feel this way.

"I'm not," he assured. "Hush now, you're distracting me."

He swung open the French doors and strode out onto the deck, walking sure-footedly down the stairs toward the lake. She blinked at the bright sunlight that shone down upon them. It made his dark hair shine with golden highlights, as if he spent all his time out in the sun. She stared at the long columns at his throat, the corded muscles making his neck thick and strong like a linebacker's. At the hollow below his Adam's apple, there was a necklace on a simple leather cord. She remembered seeing the lovely turquoise nugget and the wicked-looking tooth before. She lifted her hand to touch it, but before she could, he leaned away.

She dropped her hand.

"It's incredible."

He glanced down at her with a grimace, as if he could not wait to be rid of her.

"What kind of tooth is that?"

He raised his eyebrows. "You do not know much of animals, do you?"

"I lived in a city. Or I used to." She pointed, refusing to be distracted. "The fang?"

He smiled and shook his head in disbelief. "Claw of a grizzly."

She thought of the bear fight she had witnessed. "You killed it?"

"No, he—ah, he gave it to me." He stepped into a circle constructed of smooth river rocks and lowered her to the middle. She recognized the medicine wheel immediately.

"I'm pretty sure bears don't give away their claws voluntarily."

"You're Bear Clan?" he asked.

"Yeah." She lifted the turquoise fetish as if flashing an identification card. "But I should be Raven Clan, because they're the ones I always dream about."

The smile fell from his lips and the lines around his mouth tightened. What had she said now?

"You dream of ravens?"

She knew the legends. Ravens were symbolic to her people as a messenger from the dead.

"Only in your dreams?" His eyes narrowed as he scrutinized her, as if waiting for her to confirm some suspicion.

She thought of the raven on the windowsill of her hospital room. It was the first thing she had seen upon waking.

"Not only then."

His expression radiated astonishment.

"I see."

She suspected that he saw a great deal more than she did.

Chapter 5

Michaela knew the ceremony he performed was Native American from the tobacco he sprinkled to sanctify the ground and the fragrant smoke from a bundle of burning sage.

Most frightening was the eagle feather, which he used like a spoon to scoop out the yellow-green goop collecting in her festering wound. Each touch felt like a thread being pulled from a seam.

He collected the noxious discharge in a clay vessel and then burned it over a fire of cedar bark. Even the sweet, fragrant smoke could not cover the stench of death filling the air.

She wondered again who he was, a healer, obviously. Up until about an hour ago she believed that native cures were for the gullible and superstitious. But now she grappled with a mountain of things that she did not understand. In a few hours she had gone from certainty on many subjects to complete, jaw-dropping confusion as to what was happening to her.

When he finished the burning, he lifted his open hands to the dappled sunlight filtering through the ancient pines and chanted in a clear bass. The language was familiar, but not the words. Why hadn't she gone to classes as her mother had insisted?

Because she had been a teenager, angry at her father for leaving her and at her mother for dragging her back to nature. Now she considered the possibility that her mother believed these lessons were so vital because she knew something that Michaela did not.

Why had her mother moved them from place to place, from reservation to reservation? What had she been running from?

Sebastian's chant ended abruptly, leaving a deafening silence. Then the rustle of the pine boughs in the afternoon breeze came to her and the raucous cry of a jay as it winged through the branches.

She found him staring at her with those knowing eyes. The gaze lifted the hairs on her neck and made her stomach contract as tension coiled within her.

"How do you feel, little one?" he asked. The low rumble of his voice vibrated through her like the percussion instruments at a symphony.

Michaela gave her shoulder a tentative shrug and found the pain was gone. She sat up, a smile braking across her face, but his wary look robbed her of the momentary joy.

"It doesn't even hurt. I think I can travel now. We could go to that clinic or…" She could not quite get her mind around his suggestion of visiting the Sorceress of the North.

"Not yet."

"But why?" She pushed up, coming to a sitting position and swaying only a little.

He lifted a hand to catch her, but when she righted herself, he settled back on his haunches. "Nagi attacked your Spirit. Do you know why he pursues you?"

She shook her head, startled again that the movement brought her no pain.

"You've fixed my arm."

"No, little one. I have only drawn away the poisons, like emptying a well. They will be back."

"How do you know how to do this?"

"My father is the greatest of healers. I have inherited his power and learned how to use them from…my teachers." He rubbed his palm against the back of his neck.

"I'll take you to bed," said Sebastian.

That brought her up short.

"What?"

"So you can rest."

She glanced back toward the house. Sleep had been her enemy for so long, she instinctively fought against it.

"Let me stay out here for a little longer."

"Where would you go?"

"Perhaps down by the river."

He glanced at the line of willows. "How do you know there is a stream?"

How did she? She had seen it, hadn't she? "Willows always grow near water."

His frown showed her answer did not completely satisfy. "I will carry you."

"I can walk." She started to rise and felt a swooping dizziness rushing up to meet her.

He had her in his arms in an instant, cradling her to his broad chest with one strong arm, and he stroked her hot cheek. "The healing disturbs the balance. Lie still a moment and it will pass."

What had he done to her with that sage smoke? It was only sage and cedar—wasn't it? Hallucinogens? It would explain a lot.

"What are hallucinogens?" he asked.

"You know very well. You drugged me."

He was walking now, down a narrow path. Roots crisscrossed the exposed ground like arms stretched across the earth. They continued down a hill until the low, thick willows engulfed them. He paused, cocking his head. She turned in the same direction, seeing nothing through the entwining branches, and then she heard it, too, the crack of breaking underbrush.

She dropped the hand she had used as a visor and looked up to him for assurance.

"Bear?" she whispered, as her heartbeat accelerated to a painful hammering.

Sebastian lifted his chin and sniffed the air. "Moose. A cow and two calves."

He made a low huffing noise that brought her to complete stillness. Where had she heard that before?

Silence permeated the grove, followed an instant

later by crashing sounds as the moose and her babies exploded out of the willows in the opposite direction.

Sebastian's expression turned wistful, and she stared up at him in confusion.

"Did you just scare off a moose?"

His voice sounded bereft. "Yes."

They traveled on to the shore in silence until they broke from the cover. The path widened, revealing a fast-moving stream that cascaded around large rocks and narrowed as it rushed over a four-foot waterfall. She stared in wonder at the beauty of this place. Her head swiveled as she looked for some sign of company. At this time of year there should be fishermen lined up on both sides of the water to catch salmon, yet there was no one in either direction.

Sebastian set her on the grassy bank and crouched beside her.

"It's lovely here," she whispered, not wanting to break the silence.

He stared at the scenery as if seeing it for the first time, and then inclined his head in agreement.

"But a little lonely." She watched him for his reaction.

There was the slightest narrowing of his eyes, but he chose not to speak to her observation, instead changing the subject.

"Do you like salmon?"

"Why yes, I do."

He seemed relieved.

Sebastian sat back on his heels in a position that would have thrown Michaela's legs into muscle spasm, but he seemed relaxed. He stared out over the rushing water and began to hum. The tuneless song reminded her of a chant, and she wondered why he would pray now. Gradually her arms and legs grew heavy. The rush of the stream and the drone of his chant lulled her. She stretched out on the bank and watched the clouds rolling past like cotton ships. She blinked and then again more slowly. On the third try she could not seem to lift her eyelids.

Sebastian smiled at the sleeping woman. He could not allow her to see him transform. He had learned from hard experience what happened when people witnessed things they did not understand. He thought of his mother and grimaced. Why had she slept with his father, if she was so repulsed by Inanoka? He knew she must have once loved his father. His presence attested to that. But then why did she hate his son?

Caught between his mother's rejection and his father's absence, Sebastian had no one.

The thought caused a familiar ache, one that had no cure. It was yet another reason why he hated this form. As a man, he suffered with sorrow and loneliness that had no place in his bear-self. As a bear he was content to wander alone. But as a man, he longed for companionship and acceptance. Weaknesses. And he was strong. Too strong to fall prey to such idiocy again. The shame of his last attempt to secure a mate made him wary. Humans hated what they did not understand. He had made a mistake that time, revealing his true nature. He would not do so again.

He glared back at the sleeping woman, with her soft skin and wide, trusting eyes. Why had he brought her here?

Sebastian felt the disturbance before he heard it and glanced to the stream.

A large gray timber wolf with luminous pale blue eyes stood at the waterline of the opposite bank. Their eyes met, but the lone male stood his ground with his nose to the air.

"Hello, Nicholas."

The wolf forded the water, transforming midstream into a tall man with short black hair and the same strange watercolor eyes, wearing only a wolf-skin cloak. When he reached the opposite bank, he wore green snakeskin cowboy boots, black jeans and a tight black T-shirt.

His friend ignored the conventions of human conversation, skipping over his greeting entirely. "What the hell are you doing?"

"What?" Sebastian tried for ignorance, but his tone came off as defensive.

Nicholas lifted his chin toward Michaela. "She's human."

His friend took a step in her direction and Sebastian moved to block him. The two faced off with Nicholas backing down first.

"You're sending out distress calls so loud I heard them two hundred miles away."

Sebastian frowned. He hadn't realized his turmoil was broadcasting to other Inanoka.

Nicholas's exasperation changed with mercurial speed into suspicion.

"Oh, no. You said you'd never… You stood right there and told me to hamstring you if you ever changed your mind."

"I haven't."

Nicholas slapped his own forehead. "You brought her here. Smells like you need some help to me."

"I haven't slept with her."

Nicholas rolled his eyes like a teenager instead of a man more than a century old. "Yet."

Sebastian sighed and then told his friend the circumstances preceding his houseguest's arrival.

"And you're planning to keep her?"

"To release her would be to reveal the existence of the Spirit World."

"If that's all, just let her die. No one would find her."

Sebastian rubbed his nose and glanced at Michaela, sleeping peacefully on the bank. Her peace depended on his protection. He could just walk away. Nicholas was right. No one would ever find her out here.

He rejected the idea so forcefully his stomach muscles contracted. He would keep her. Sebastian glared at his friend.

Nicholas pointed an accusing finger. "I knew it."

"I'm keeping her."

"Temporarily," Nicholas qualified, and waited for the concurrence that never came. He gave a sigh of resignation. "What do you know of her people?"

His friend could track anyone anywhere in the world, if he had their scent. It was his gift.

"There was an old man at the cabin where I found her."

Sebastian told him where Michaela lived. Perhaps he could find a scent trail there.

"If she has living kin, I'll find him." Nicholas rubbed a finger under his nose. "What if they're looking for her?"

Sebastian stared coldly back toward the sleeping woman, then met his friend's troubled gaze. "Then she'll be just one more missing person. The wilderness is a dangerous place, far more dangerous than humans can possibly imagine."

"Let's try to keep it that way," said Nicholas.

The wolf turned to go and then changed his mind, facing Sebastian once more.

"Nagi can come at you as anything, anytime. Possession is nothing to him."

"I know."

"You sure you want to do this?"

Sebastian stared, unable to explain the irrational choice.

"If you're doing this thing, you need Bess. She understands females and the Spirit World."

"That jabbering feather duster? No, thanks."

Nicholas turned serious. "You are in over your head, friend. If Nagi wants her, he'll get her."

"Not if I can help it."

"You can't."

"Goodbye, Nicholas."

Chapter 6

Sebastian rose, casting off his human form. The misshapen clothing transformed into his perfectly fitting hide as he sank to all fours to amble up the bank to his favorite fishing place. The thick red bodies rushed and jumped before him. With his claw, he lunged, slapping one large king salmon after another far up on the bank. His reflexes and much practice made his movements supple and quick.

He lifted his head and bellowed, transforming to his human form. He tied a river reed around the salmon tail and hoisted them over his back. Only when the wet scales touched his back did he recall he was again naked except for his bearskin cloak.

He touched the cloak, shifting it to his customary

necklace and the clothing he wore before fishing. He chanted as he walked, asking for the woman to wake from her healing sleep. As he drew near, she stretched. The action sent her into an arched position that made her breasts strain against the lacy fabric.

He stopped short as his body reacted to the sight. The fish slid from his hands as his groin pulsed to life, his erection straining against the denim fabric of his jeans. What in the name of Maka was this? He turned to the water, feeling as if the thermally heated water rushed through his veins. He breathed deep, struggling against the raw need she raised with just the arching of her back. It was several moments before he turned back and retrieved his salmon.

He found her sitting up and smiling at him. Then a look of utter astonishment crossed her face.

"Was I asleep?"

"For a little while."

"But that's not possible. I didn't have a nightmare. I always…but?"

He smiled. She looked so astounded. Wonderment glowed from her upturned face. And then he noted the circles beneath her eyes and felt a jolt of anger so strong it caused him to drop his catch again. How long had Nagi been haunting this woman?

"My presence insures your dreams are sweet."

Her lovely smile was his reward.

"Thank you," she said. "For protecting me."

The determination of his resolve to defend her worried Sebastian almost as much as the thought of her enemies. What had begun as a need to protect the world of the supernatural from men had changed. It was foolish. He knew she only accepted him now because she did not know what he was. Her smile, her gratitude, rested on the continuity of this illusion. To keep her, he must best her enemies and he must hide his other self.

She glanced at the ground beside him.

"You went fishing!"

He glanced at the salmon now lying on the bank.

"Oh, lovely. I'm starved."

He wanted only to pull that delicate top from her body and kiss her soft skin. The veracity of the impulse made him wary. He reminded himself that he was not the only one with secrets. It was best to move with caution when on unfamiliar ground.

"How was your rest?"

She gave a tentative flex of her injured arm and then cast him a sleepy smile. He needed to touch her again, needed to know if she shared these desires.

He sank to his knees before her and lifted a hand, reaching.

She scuttled back like a crab. "You smell like fish."

He dropped his hand and recaptured the salmon. "Come."

She rose beside him with no sign of weakness. The sleep had restored her balance for the time being. But he knew that the Spirit Wound continued to grow within her, choking her like a grapevine.

She fell in behind him as they retraced their steps. This was good, as he did not have to watch her hips sway and beckon as she walked. But still he could smell her rich, enticing scent. He wanted to bury his face in her neck and inhale the fragrance of her hair. Never had anything smelled as good as Michaela.

"Where is your fishing gear?" she asked.

He smiled. "I left it by the river."

Back at the lakeshore, he filleted the fish, leaving the skin and innards for scavengers. His lodge had a propane stove, the fuel brought in on the ice trail in the winter. Solar panels supplied the power for hot water and electricity. He even had satellite television and a GPS phone. His one additional concession was a refrigerator, though he still had a spring house. Most of all he preferred fresh food.

He held open the door and waited for her, anxious to show off his ability in the kitchen. He found himself looking forward to her companionship. For so long he had eaten all his meals alone. It was a choice. He preferred his own company and could think of no one with whom he wished to share his time, until now.

Before long he had wine open and had poured two generous glasses three-quarters full. He spiced his corn bread mix with a can of chopped jalapenos to give the biscuits some zip. He set the lumpy batter to sizzling in the deep cast-iron skillet, then spiced the salmon, pulling out the marinade to add just before serving. He left her to tend to the bread as he stepped onto the deck to start the fish.

At his return, Michaela abandoned her post in favor of a stool at the granite countertop, where she watched him set out plates, silverware and linen napkins. She was sipping her wine and studying him. Her attention distracted him, but the bread was rescued before it was overly brown.

He arranged an enormous portion of fish beside a hunk of corn bread and then set it before her. Then he topped off their wine before loading his plate and joining her.

He usually ate in the formal dining room looking out over the lake. But everything was in easy reach from here and she'd said she was hungry. He added canned peaches as an afterthought, dumping the slippery, syrupy fruit into a bowl and adding a large spoon. He told himself he just wanted her strong enough for the journey to Kanka, but then why did he keep taking sidelong looks to see if she enjoyed what he provided for her?

The next time he cast her a glance, he found her studying him. The unease returned.

"Sebastian, how do you do it? Travel on the wind, I mean."

He lowered his fork and regarded her. "Do you wish to return to your life one day?"

Her eyes widened in surprise. "Of course."

"Then you must not know these things."

"But I don't understand."

"And so I can return you to your path. Once you understand, you must stay with me."

The prickling of her skin told her this was not an idle threat. Would he kill her? Surely he could have done that already just by leaving her behind.

"Why did you help me?"

"I did not want Nagi to have you."

She raised her eyebrows again, urging him to continue, and her patience was rewarded.

"And because you intrigue me." He sipped his wine, slowly lowering it back to its place. "Nagi has his world and we ours. Yet he hunts you." He studied her with an intent, searching gaze. "Why?"

"I don't know."

"Have you killed anyone?"

She blinked in shock at the matter-of-fact tone of his voice. He might well have asked her to pass him the salt.

"What?"

"Murder," he clarified.

She lowered her corn bread, feeling her appetite abandon her. "Of course not."

"What evil have you done, then?"

She shifted uncomfortably as she recalled the legend—if it was a legend.

At death, all ghosts walked the Spirit Road. But before entering the Spirit World, the soul faced Hihankara, the withered old crone who guarded the path. If the soul did not bear the correct mark, she pushed it from the road where it fell into the Circle of Ghosts.

"I am *not* evil."

"Nagi does not pursue the innocent."

She had no answer to this, the most bizarre conversation of her life.

"Who are your parents?"

"My mother was Maggie Proud. She lived in the cabin near where you found me."

"The old woman?"

"Yes. Have you met her?" Michaela held her breath as she waited for the answer.

"I have seen her."

Her mother had told her the place was magical, but Michaela had never believed it.

"What of your father?"

"I don't remember him."

Sebastian set his plate aside. "Why?"

"He left us when I was young. I don't know much about him." Because her mother would not speak of him. It had been an ongoing source of conflict between them. She did not even remember what he looked like.

He had gone long ago and that hurt most of all. She tried to pretend that she did not need the man who did not need her. But secretly she had longed for him to come back to them. He never did. And now she didn't want him to. She didn't need him or any man. It was easier to rely on herself.

She lifted her gaze to find him staring. "He just left, you know. Happens sometimes."

"I don't think so. What was his name?"

"Michael Proud."

"You are named to honor him."

Michaela dropped her gaze and reached for the wine, draining her glass.

"Do you know where to find him?" asked Sebastian.

"Last I heard he was in Nebraska. He stopped writing to us a long time ago." Yet she had waited for him year after year. Michaela had had several dreams in which he was dead. She'd had enough of this topic. "Why do you live all alone?"

He hesitated, then seemed to decide to indulge her. "I do not like company."

She glanced to the living room and the massive bookshelves that stretched up and out on either side of the fireplace. He had a plasma television and iPod set up in a speaker system. "But you have so many books, music, television. They are all company."

"But require no attention. I do not have to feed or water them and they are easy to silence."

She threw down her linen napkin. "If I am such an inconvenience, take me back."

"I cannot."

"Why?"

"Because your wound is dangerous."

"Contagious, you mean?"

"No, I mean it cannot be explained in your world."

He did not want others to see her injury and he could not heal it. She did not believe his fairy tale about the sorceress. That meant… A cold wave of fear rushed through her as her eyes widened. What a stupid little fool she was, sitting here, drinking his wine.

"You're waiting for me to die out here."

He did not deny it.

The wineglass fell from her numb fingers, shattering on the stone counter. "Oh, my God!"

"Michaela, listen. I admit I considered it, but I have already given you my aid and protection."

She trembled from head to toe, unable to even speak past the terror.

"If I had intended to kill you, there are easier ways."

Was that meant to reassure her? She gasped at the clinical way he thought of her. She knew better than to trust a man. Her father had taught her that lesson early on. But she had no choice, no other option but death.

"Take me home this instant."

Chapter 7

"Please." Michaela was astonished she could speak past the fingers of terror constricting her throat. "Please take me home."

"Not until I know why Nagi seeks you."

Were his words a trick to reassure her?

She didn't care. This reason was so much more appealing than the thought that he meant to wait with her until she died. He offered hope and she snatched at it with both hands, not caring if his version was fact or illusion.

"How do we do that?"

"Discover what you have that he wants or…"

His hesitation did nothing to comfort. "What?"

"Wait until he comes back."

She went pale at that. "It will come back?"

He nodded. "All you've told me indicates he will.

Nagi can't reach you as a Spirit, but he can possess other creatures."

"Like the bear."

"Yes."

She glanced about, searching for the next attacker, hating herself for suddenly swallowing the nonsense her mother talked. Nagi could have possessed that moose or…her eyes fell upon her protector…or Sebastian.

She inched away.

He reached out and she dodged his hand, but he easily captured her wrist, dragging her from her perch. He held her trapped between his knees and the granite counter as he stared at her with those knowing eyes. She tried to escape but gave up the attempt as futile. The man was a mountain of brawn. She wasn't going anywhere until he said so. She did the only thing left to her, she stilled and stared defiantly into his eyes, but it did not matter, for this time she felt the connection of his mind to hers.

He remained motionless for several moments and then released her. She fell back into the counter, gripping the smooth polished edge.

Sebastian did not try to recapture her as she put the stool between them.

"He already tried to possess me," he said, "and failed."

She stared at him. "He tried?"

He nodded.

"But how did you stop him?"

"That's complicated."

She recognized the expression. She was intruding on his precious secrets again. But Nagi was stalking her. That gave her the right to know—even though the information she discovered would likely scare the daylights out of her.

He wouldn't tell her. That was clear, but it wouldn't stop her from trying her damnedest to uncover what she was up against.

She laid a hand over his. He flashed her a questioning look but allowed it. She recognized it was the first time she had initiated this contact and hoped she might see his thoughts as he so easily read hers.

"My mother said ghosts had to be exorcised by a medicine man."

"Ghosts, yes. Once a creature is possessed, the ghost will usually not leave unless forced by a shaman or by death of the host. But Nagi is no mere ghost. He has much power."

He spoke the truth. She instinctively knew it.

Michaela ignored his worried look. It made him appear as if he cared about her welfare more than his secret. "Well, then, why does he keep popping up to terrify me when he could just take possession of me and walk me into traffic?"

Sebastian raised his brows as she registered his astonishment. He hadn't thought of that, but she had. He gave her an approving smile, as if impressed.

"I don't know. Perhaps he cannot. But why?"

"You're asking me?"

The heat and energy of their contact made it difficult for her to think. Powerful images filled her mind. She saw herself stretched out naked on his wide, bare chest. She closed her eyes at the lure of flesh pressed to flesh. She jerked back her hand and scowled at him.

"You wanted to know my thoughts," he said. "Now you do."

The look he cast her was so primal, so hungry, she braced as she faced a different kind of threat.

Instead of lunging at her, he reached for his wine, finishing the contents in one sensual swallow.

He set the glass beside her shattered one and walked to the windows. "He comes to you often?"

Apparently he was not ready to act on impulse.

She released her breath and resisted the urge to follow him. "Only in my dreams, until today."

"When you saw the bear?" He seemed to brace himself for her answer, planting his feet and clasping his hands behind his back.

"I saw him in the kitchen window first."

He glanced back at her, one brow quirked. "Does he speak to you?"

She nodded.

"What does he say?" he asked.

"In my dreams he says things like, 'I can see you.'"

He turned, his brow knit in concern. "See you?"

She walked as far as the couch, then sat on the armrest, facing him. He looked magnificent framed against the vista behind him. She wished she were a painter and could capture him here, like this. Michaela recognized belatedly that he waited for her to elaborate. How long had she been sitting here mooning at him like a teenager waiting at the stage door?

"What? Oh, yes, as if it couldn't see me before," she said. "Another time it said, 'I've found you.'"

"How long has it been visiting your dreams?"

"Since the accident." She glanced at her strange protector. He acted like some king of surveying his territory. She could not resist joining him there. "I was on a bike trail in a park near Vancouver. That's where I lived until my mom got sick. But I ran into a bad patch, lost control and hit my head. The doctors said if I hadn't worn my helmet I'd be dead." She stopped beside him and lifted her hair back so he could see the tiny scar. "Pressure cut. Anyway, my friends called for help and I spent five days in intensive care. When I woke up…" She hesitated, thinking what had happened next was too bizarre to relate. She didn't tell people this part, but neither did she travel on whirlwinds or wrestle with bears. Michaela drew a breath to gather her resolve. If she was going to buy in to this madness, she might as well tell him all of it. "I woke up and there was a raven on my windowsill at the hospital."

"A messenger from the Spirit World. When did your mother die?"

Michaela's eyes burned as they always did when she fought tears. "A month later. It was very aggressive, the cancer. I moved in with her and—" she shrugged "—I stayed after she passed."

"Did she follow the old ways?"

"Oh, yeah."

His gaze seemed to judge her and find her lacking. She lifted her chin in defiance.

"But you do not." He made it sound like a condemnation.

She felt the need to defend herself. "My mother was always trying to get me to listen to legends and join the tribe." Michaela looked out over the glassy blue waters before her. What had Maggie known of this?

"You should have listened. You would have been better prepared for what will come."

Michaela stiffened at the rebuke. "I don't believe in ghosts."

"But they believe in you."

She found her breathing coming too quickly. "But ghosts are just souls that have not crossed over to the other side."

He shook his head. "Not all. Some are what remains of evil men and women after their bodies die. They are greedy for the life they have lost—vengeful creatures. Nagi collects these souls from earth, like a bounty hunter, keeping humans safe from the dangerous criminals."

She shifted uncomfortably. It was her mother's variety of ghosts, not the Christian version. Ghosts were to be feared, avoided and protected against.

He eyed her critically. "I begin to think that Nagi wants your soul. But he cannot take a life. It is his misery, to wait until the evil ones finish their deplorable lives before collecting them. But I do not find you evil."

Her mother had always said she was special, but all mothers said that. When odd things happened, Michaela ignored the creepy stuff that she didn't understand. She could disregard them no longer.

"How do I get rid of him?"

"By discovering why it pursues you. Nagi does not stalk the innocent. So his actions confuse me. I want to hear more about the hospital."

She gazed out at clouds just beginning to turn pink against the blue autumn sky and dodged the question.

"Where is this place?"

"A place with no name. Canadian Rockies. One of my homes."

"One of?" She lifted an eyebrow. "How many do you have?"

He shrugged.

"I don't see any roads."

Sebastian pointed to the seaplane tied to the dock as if it were a sailboat, its large pontoons looking like twin kayaks. "I use that, mostly. Lake's big enough for a landing."

He found her staring at him with lips pursed. She was obviously irritated, judging from her folded arms and lowered chin. Why, then, did he find it nearly impossible not to grab her and pull her close?

"You prefer the hurricanes."

There was no need to answer, so he did not, merely stared at her with hungry eyes taking in her high color and the clinging scent of her arousal.

"I can't believe I even said that. This whole thing is crazy." She flapped her arms like a baby duckling. "Where's the bathroom?"

"Down the hall." Sebastian pointed.

Michaela headed through the living room and out of sight. Sebastian followed her with his eyes until she disappeared and then listened to her light footfall as she slowed at the bathroom. He heard the click and then the sound of water running. He switched his attention to the lake. His hearing was good, good enough to hear the ground squirrel burrowing in the roots of the ponderosa pine on the south end of the deck. But it was his sense of smell that was most acute, which was how he could smell the pine-scented soap she now used. He closed his eyes and imagined what it would be like to nuzzle at her freshly washed wrist.

He cast his gaze like a net over the water. Sebastian had placed his home on the eastern shore of the secluded lake so as to take in the sunset. The water was so calm this evening that the lavender clouds were fringed in scarlet, reflected in mirror image upon the still lake. He saw such things as a bear, but their magnificence escaped him. He took in the moment, savoring it, letting the tranquillity fill a part of him he had not known needed filling.

He sought a view, not to search for game or guard against intruders, but for this. He threw open the doors and breathed deep of the sweet, clean air.

Down the hall the running water ceased. Was she coming? His body twitched in anticipation. How could he miss her when she had been out of his sight for only a few moments? Yet he recognized the eagerness and the anticipation, but forced himself to keep his eyes upon the still waters.

She was human, and human females were the only creatures on earth powerful enough to hurt him.

Chapter 8

Michaela looked longingly at the shower and then at herself in the large mirror hanging over the sink. Dirt flecked her pink camisole and ragged denim shirt and her hair fell in a wild tangle. She washed her face and arms. Rummaging in the drawer, she did locate a comb, making use of it before heading back to Sebastian. She had not even cleared the hallway when she sensed him, his attention on the vista but his focus entirely on her approach.

She paused. This was new, wasn't it? She had always known when someone was staring at her. That was some deep instinct of the hunted, but this was different.

He had left the doors to the deck open and now stood at the rail. She went to him, stopping right behind him, and following her instinct, she rested a hand on his arm. He glanced at her hand but allowed the contact.

He seemed deeply troubled by her. Worried over her wound, perhaps, and his inability to heal her.

His gaze rose to hers, intensified, his pupils dilated, and he gave her a look that hummed of unfulfilled desire. He wanted her.

Her blood turned to quicksilver, flashing through her hot and cold as she responded to his unspoken desire. Sebastian had not made any physical advances toward her, but now she understood the intense internal battle he waged not to do so. It was a battle he was losing.

But how did she know?

She stared at the bandage on her arm. Somehow this was related.

She felt the heat of his gaze as it swept down her body and then flashed back to her eyes. His expression most resembled a grimace of someone stoically avoiding some great temptation, as if she offered food to a fasting monk. She should be cautious. Wine or no wine, this man, or whatever the hell he was, was dangerous and he didn't like her, felt somehow threatened by her.

That was ridiculous.

"What threat could I possibly be to you?"

He drew away. "You make me want things I cannot have."

What things? What couldn't he have?

"I don't understand."

"And that is best for now."

She resisted the urge to kick him in the shins, but instead exhaled her frustration. "I would like to take a shower."

He drew back as if she were suddenly contagious.

"Do you think there is something I could wear?" She motioned toward the missing sleeves. "You know, afterward?"

"No."

"No, you don't have any, or no, I can't wear them."

"I have no clothing."

"That's ridiculous. A T-shirt, for heaven's sake."

He shook his head. The man had white wine and fine crystal but didn't own a pair of socks. She'd heard of traveling light, but this was ridiculous.

"Fine. Can I take a shower?"

"Of course."

She turned and his voice halted her. "Afterward I will replace the bandage."

"All right."

He beckoned with his head and stalked away, moving through the house, down the hall and into a bedroom. She followed, pausing in the doorway as she gasped in surprise. She did not know what she expected, but not this fairy-tale bed. The headboard had been carved of blond wood by a consummate craftsman, but instead of garlands of flowers or cherubs, realistically carved animals sprang from the wide expanse of wood alive with character. A raven perched on each of the four posts, beaks raised and open, as if calling to one another. On the headboard, flanking foxes appeared beside mountain goats and two baying wolves, and in the center sat a bear looking smug and satisfied by his central position.

"What a lovely bed."

"You'll sleep here." His words made it sound like an

order instead of an invitation. "And don't leave the lodge unless I am with you."

Her eyes narrowed at this. His ultimatum made this lovely mountain lodge seem more prison than sanctuary. She was now well aware of the dangers surrounding her, though she had trouble believing all of what was happening. She wanted to dismiss it, but she just could not. For an instant, she wished this was a hallucination. Then she would have the freedom to do as she liked instead of the responsible thing. For example, she could rest her hand on his arm and lean closer to him for a kiss.

He strode across the room, past the chair upholstered in green velvet, past the simple bureau, stopping at the threshold.

"Call when you are finished and I will see to the wound." He seemed to want to say something more but instead he clamped his lips closed, turned and stalked away with more speed than grace.

She stared after him, fascinated by the primal aura of supremacy radiating from him. Who was he and how did he have such powers? Mulling the possibilities, she explored her room. There was a walk-in closet, devoid of even a single hanger. She turned to the dresser, opening one empty drawer after another. It looked more like a model home than a real one. It certainly wasn't lived in, at least not in the way she understood.

She closed the last drawer and glanced out the bare window devoid of curtains or blinds. What time was it? She found not one clock in the room, and she'd failed to put her watch on this morning. She studied the sky. The long summer days and northern latitude meant that sunset came slowly. But even now the sky turned a deeper blue and the shadows grew long on the ground. Soon she would see her reflection in this dark window. She stepped back from the pane and glanced at the bed. Then she would have to close her eyes and sleep.

Would the ghost attack her again, or did Sebastian's protection extend to this place, as well?

Michaela backed from the room, recalling the shadow creature she'd seen in the glass. Nagi? Sebastian said so and she began to believe it was possible.

Shaking off her apprehension, she headed to the bathroom. A bracing shower would chase the shadows away. She closed the door behind her and stripped out of her jeans and tops, leaving the bandage in place. She told herself it was to protect the wound, but in reality she did not want to see the charred flesh again.

Sebastian's guest bathroom had a travertine floor, flecked granite countertops and a raised basin sink made of black marble. The shower echoed the travertine and was trimmed with a small black rectangular tile that had some kind of animal track stamped into its surface to make it appear as if a creature had run the perimeter in wet clay. She fingered the indentation and thought it most resembled a bear paw.

She turned on the taps, praying for hot water. Her prayers were answered as steam rose around her. Michaela turned to her reflection and stiffened. She grasped a bath towel from the rack and draped the towel over the oval mirror before stripping out of her panties and stepping under the warm spray.

Paradise, she thought, as she turned in a full circle.

* * *

Outside the door, Sebastian pressed a hand to the solid wood and let his mind wander as he heard her sigh with pleasure. The insistent throbbing ache at his groin intensified at the symphony of the water jets drenching her skin.

"The hell with this," he growled, and headed out the double doors and down the hill; then, without pausing, he splashed into the lake. He dove into the water, changing his clothing into the simple necklace as he submerged. He needed to keep his skin with him, and the circlet around his neck was most efficient. He surfaced, letting the water stream from his heated flesh. Then he dove again and swam with swift, powerful strokes, trying in vain to work away the tension building relentlessly inside him. The exercise did not rid him of the desire. This had never happened before.

He stood in the chest-deep water, his feet sinking into the ooze. Was this what his father felt for his mother? Did he have this same unquenchable thirst to possess her?

He huffed, shaking his head in misery. He had to be rid of her, but already he wanted to keep her. This was new territory for him. Nicholas had managed relations with human females, had been with many human females, including a naturalist he'd lived with for over a month, but when he'd found himself growing fond, he'd left her. Brevity prevented attachments. When Sebastian had asked what he did if he grew fond of her, Nicholas had laughed. Sebastian knew it was vital to keep humans at arm's length if one wanted to prevent offspring. For a human to carry the child of a Skinwalker, she must first have fallen in love with him. She could not be taken by force, and consent was not enough. Perhaps it was the Great Spirit's way of limiting his kind.

Sebastian still worried. His existence and Nicholas's were proof that some humans could love Halflings. Nicholas was wise to set these women back upon their path, unharmed and unaware of what he was.

Sebastian had been with Michaela for little more than one full circle of the sun, and yet already she had seen the whirlwind and a Supernatural Spirit.

He admitted the truth. He wanted Michaela so badly it tortured him, and not just for a night. He did not believe he could work her out of his system. He envied his friend's cavalier attitude and detachment, something Sebastian never managed.

Unlike the wolf, deception was contrary to his nature. He understood he could not tell Michaela, yet to take her without telling her was deceitful. He would not trick a woman as his father had done to his mother, not only because it was wrong, but because he wanted the woman who accepted him to know him for himself.

Once he thought he had found such a woman.

He had not thought of Anoki for many decades. She was long dead now, which was another reason Inanoka did not often take human companions—their short span of years. Nicholas said it didn't matter if you only stayed one night. But it did.

Sebastian dunked his head.

This was the legacy of his father, the curse of the supernatural that Sebastian was determined would die with him. If any more unfortunate souls were to be born to walk through life alone they would not come from him.

In his early days, far south of here, when Sebastian still felt connected to his tribe but after his change and then his banishment, he had come back a year later for Anoki. She had loved him or said she loved him and he naively thought that nothing could alter her love.

He had been so certain that she would accept him even when his own family would not. He could still hear her screams and feel the sting of the rocks she threw to drive him off. The humiliation had been enough to penetrate even his thick skull. No woman was strong enough to love a Skinwalker.

He glanced toward the house. Michaela asked why he lived alone. The truth was hard. If his own wife could not accept him, who could?

Sebastian's thoughts were interrupted by the sound of the water pump switching off. She was out of the shower. Before stopping to think, he left the lake, pausing only to shake the water droplets from his skin.

What did she think was happening to her?

He read her fear and it troubled him. It was wrong to cause fear in another creature; even when hunting he killed quickly and mercifully. But this feeling was more than not wanting to frighten her. He wanted to comfort, protect, claim. Never in his solitary life had he had such impulses.

He stood on the soft moss that grew thick below the porch, wearing only his claw necklace. But this wouldn't do. He pictured the clothing. An instant later the garments assembled over his skin. He was dressed, though the jeans were slightly damp. He glanced down at his bare feet.

"The hell with it." He stalked to the stairs. The pads of his feet were tough from going without shoes and he was as sure-footed as a goat.

He reached the deck as she left the bathroom. He heard the door click open and smelled the humid air that billowed down the hallway. She had found a new fragrance. He sniffed the air and recognized the scent of lemon oil. It was some lotion. He recalled the white bottle, but it smelled different as it reacted with her own chemistry, changing it into something sensual and erotic as all hell.

He growled again.

"Sebastian?" Her call was low and tentative. But something in her tone beckoned.

He was not at all sure what would happen now. She called to him on so many levels. How long could he resist her?

He stalked forward, homing in on her scent, tracking his prey. If she were wise, she would run. Instead, he found Michaela peeking down the hallway from the bathroom. Her smile died on her lips as she spotted him striding toward her and apprehension bloomed on her features.

"Ah, I've finished."

She backed up as he filled the doorway. What was she wearing? He stared at the fluffy white towel she had wrapped around herself in a tempting package. He grasped hold of the edge of the cloth, fighting the urge to tug. The bulk of twisted terry cloth pressed her breasts together, creating an enticing line of cleavage. The edge of the towel cut across her slim thighs. He glanced at her inviting legs, picturing them wrapped around his hips as he plunged into her warm, wet body.

"You call to me dressed in this?"

She flushed and dropped her gaze.

"You said you have no other clothes. I didn't want to put on my dirty ones." She rubbed the bandage uneasily. "You wanted to change this?"

"Not anymore." He was having trouble recalling anything but the inviting smell of her warm, damp skin.

She crossed her arms before her and he stared at the sodden gauze, feeling guilty for his primal thoughts. He squeezed his hands into fists to gain control before reaching to unwind the bandage. What would he find beneath?

The moment he touched her, he had her thoughts once more. The crazy jumble brought him up short.

Fear and longing battled like supernatural beings for control of her will.

She grasped the wrapping and unwound the bandage until it fell away. She was outwardly brave as she gazed at the wound, revealing none of her inner turmoil.

He shifted his attention to the four-inch gash that neither scabbed nor bled. He was relieved to see none of the otherworldly green glow, but troubled that there was no sign of healing.

He felt her eyes on him as she sought reassurance. Sebastian struggled to think of something optimistic. "There is no evidence of Nagi's mark."

"The strangest part is that it doesn't hurt. Why is that?" She moved her arm up and down to show him.

He knew the reason.

His eyes narrowed and he released her, unsure if she could read any part of his thoughts.

Nagi killed the nerves along with the flesh. If he could not heal the damage, the wound would kill her. Sebastian's stomach constricted with the force of his next realization. He did not want to lose this woman.

He met her gaze, noting the tension around her mouth and recognizing her need for some measure of hope. It was then he knew he would lie for her sake.

"My healing gifts are strong." He tried not to squirm at the relief that glowed in her smile.

His own mouth went dry.

Where were the blasted bandages?

He found them and set to work, gingerly wrapping to avoid grazing her bare flesh. He had never read the thoughts of a human before and could not explain this development.

He finished the knot and glanced up to find her green eyes pinning him.

For the first and only time in his life, he felt hunted. What was she playing at to give him such a direct stare?

Had she been a male he would have accepted the threat and clouted him, but from a female, this aggressive gaze meant something entirely different. Or at least he thought it did.

And she gave this summoning look to him. He could barely keep the hope from stealing his breath.

She wanted him, didn't she? A touch would give him the answer. He leaned closer.

But then he remembered, she didn't know what he was, not entirely, at least. It was why she still desired him. The realization dampened some of his need, but it did not extinguish, clinging tenaciously to his desire as a flame in a rainstorm. Slowly the desire gained ground.

It was not the only time in his life he wished that he were merely human. The first was when his mother saw him transform and had run from him screaming. He'd been an adolescent and not able to fully control his powers.

Now he was. So Michaela would not know. The only question was whether to deceive her or leave.

Her smile made him dizzy with longing.

"Thank you." She indicated the bandage.

"You should rest," he said, hoping she would leave him now before he acted on the promise in her eyes.

"I'm not sleepy."

He heard the lie in her voice and understood. Perhaps this was not so much about desire as it was her fears. "It won't come while you are under my protection."

Her eyes assessed him.

He stood his ground. "Go to bed, Michaela."

She hesitated. He reached out and brushed her cheek with the palm of his hand. He drew a breath at the sharp desire that leaped out at him. It vibrated from her like hoofbeats through dry ground. But that was not all—he read uncertainty, as well.

She knew he was dangerous, some kind of "other" being. It was why she hesitated. It would not be difficult to push her to one direction or the other.

She stared at his mouth, wanting his kiss. He met her gaze.

"You're sure?"

She knew what he was asking. He sensed it. The

tension shimmered between them in waves like heat off asphalt, and he found his uncertainty drain away. He would kiss her. Even if she retreated, he would have this at least. He would taste her lips and feel the warmth of her tongue glide over his.

He bent toward her, looming as he captured her, pressing her forward, preventing her escape and realizing that she did not want to. Instead, she lifted to her toes, straining to reach him. It was a gift he had never expected.

Chapter 9

As Sebastian's lips met hers, she poured herself onto him like warm honey, molding to every contour. Warm, damp terry cloth rubbed against his chest. He trembled at the wave of need the contact awakened—hers and his, wrapping around each other like vines.

Michaela's lips trembled as he explored them, nibbling first and then stroking with his tongue. Her mouth opened and he slipped his tongue against hers, tasting the mint of mouthwash. The scent of pine clung to her damp skin and he breathed her in.

The closer he drew her, the more her body accommodated his intrusion, and the harder he pressed against her. She lifted a leg to grip him, bringing his erection in contact with her sex. He paused, trying to clear the red haze of lust. He drew back and shook his head, but her fingers twined in his hair, insisting.

Her mind barraged him with messages, thumping against him like a storm on the beach. She wanted him to stroke her breast, touch her sex, kiss her lips.

He drew one hand from her back and grabbed the front of her towel, bunching it in his fist and meeting her eyes with a challenge of his own. She lifted her chin and he yanked the terry-cloth sheath from her body.

He held it before them like the scalp of an enemy taken in battle, then cast it to the floor.

She stood before him wearing nothing but the spiraling circlet of gauze around one upper arm. He stared into her green eyes, measuring the heat, flashing like the fire of a cut emerald caught in sunlight. Her pulse beat through the two vessels that flanked the slim column of her throat. He longed to kiss her where her neck and shoulder joined.

Her fast breathing caused her full breasts to rise and fall. He found the invitation irresistible.

He reached and she met him halfway. His fingers splayed, flattening the soft, pliant flesh of her breasts. Her head dropped back as she groaned with pleasure at the kneading pressure of his hands. The tender flesh of her breasts responded, growing firm to his touch. Her nipples beaded into tight knots in his palms, making him greedy to taste her.

She wanted him to. That thought came through most insistently.

He kissed, but now she wanted his mouth on her neck. He complied, lifting her to the counter to give him better access to her throat. Sebastian has set his counters high, but not quite high enough for this. Her thoughts transmitted the cold stone against her heated flesh and her need for him to suckle at her.

He hesitated, and she pressed her hands against the back of his head, insisting. She could not force him to do anything; in fact, he could break free with very little effort if he chose to. Instead, he found that he wanted to do as she bid—hungered to please her in all things.

She desired it, so he complied, slipping his hands around her and stroking her nipple with his tongue as he grazed her sweet flesh with his teeth. His rising need swirled within him, fueled by her cries of delight.

He knew she wanted him inside her, begged him silently in her mind. He paused at this new need for the friction of their joining. She was fragile, this female. It had been many years since he had taken a human. Back in the days when he was young, before he understood that all relations would be brief and end badly, back when he still held hope, he had taken many women, confidently, repeatedly.

But not like this. And never before had he been able to know a female's thought. Why now—why with this woman?

He drew back to stare a moment at the loveliness of her form, dazzled by the smooth, firm flesh. He still held her and so read the change in her emotions. There was hesitance now and doubt as modesty invaded her desire like an intruder in her home. He did not understand this human shortcoming and so dipped to brush her nipple with his lips.

At the instant of contact, a cry escaped her parted lips and her head dropped back to expose the long column of her neck. Had he not been touching her, connected to her in some way he did not understand, he would have halted immediately at her cry. But it was not pain that caused her to call out, but pleasure. He felt it keenly. Michaela leaned still closer, offering this bounty to him. The bliss he gave to her quivered through her like a living thing and he felt it all. He did not understand what was happening or pause to wonder why.

My neck, kiss my neck.

She wanted him there and he moved to obey her command. Never had he thought to do what another compelled him. Most of the time he did the opposite, but this woman's pleasure fueled his like two logs laid across the same inferno.

She tugged at his shirt, sending a message of frustration at this barrier between the warm, intoxicating contact of his flesh against hers. He lifted his hand to his throat, touching the necklace and his clothing vanished. Behind him on the floor lay his cloak. Without it he was trapped forever in human form. But he left it there, parted from him for the only time since he first grew his hide on his own back, left it there unprotected to have this woman whose call was louder than the beating of the Thunderbird's wings.

He groaned with pleasure at the velvety feel of her thighs splaying open to allow him between them. She wanted him to take her now. He grasped her hips, holding her so she could not escape him. He lifted his gaze to find her staring at him. Her eyes beckoned, making promises he did not understand. But he accepted her offer, positioning himself to join his flesh to hers. She leaned back as he slid into the liquid folds of her, thrusting his hips so he glided into her warm, tight passage. The collision of his pleasure, combined with hers, nearly buckled his knees, and he paused before fully entering her, absorbing the sensations that soared through them.

Her impatience hit him an instant before she rocked her hips, taking what he had denied. Their hips collided with a satisfying bump. Her legs wrapped around him, locking them together in an intimate embrace. He faced her, still gazing into her astonishing eyes.

The counter was too low for him to have her as he would like, so he dragged her up into his arms.

She exhaled and gripped his shoulders. She did not like this change, fearing he would drop her. He nearly laughed at her thoughts of her weight and his ability as he straightened his powerful legs, lifting her still higher.

He drew her near until her breasts pressed to him and his lips touched the shell of her ear as he whispered to her. "I can hold you. Trust me."

The doubt flickered and died as she released her grip, leaning away, extending her arms at his shoulders as he grasped her hips and rocked her, bringing her body up and down on his shaft. She gasped and he felt the welling, tightening preparation inside her. Her arms fell away as her head dropped back. He gripped her ribs and moved with greater force; the delicious feel of her heels digging deep into the muscles of his flanks encouraged him to greater speed.

She was coming. He felt the rippling contractions begin at her core and roll outward in sweeping waves, like a current caused by a heavy stone dropped in still waters.

Her pleasure peaked, overwhelmed her and triggered his release. The sheer sensual joy of this moment of mutual bliss shocked him. Never in his entire existence had he experienced such physical gratification.

She stared at him with eyes rounded in astonishment. He could think of nothing else to do but to gather her to his body and hold her. She curled against his chest, her legs going slack. He did not lower her to the floor as she hoped, but collected her in his arms, carrying her to her bedchamber, where he lay with her upon the downy coverlet. The soft pillow of the thing made him understand why she preferred this to fur.

He kissed Michaela's forehead and her cheeks, while he gently stroked her hair, astonished at the silken texture. The quality rivaled a mink's, though was not as thick. But softer, oh, yes, much softer.

She sighed and her eyes drifted closed. Fear brought them open again, chasing away the lethargy and contentment. She dreaded sleep, worried Nagi would find her.

"Do not fear him. I will protect you."

She met his gaze and nodded solemnly. She believed him, and he wondered at her faith in him. He forced a smile.

He could protect her sleep. But he could not keep Nagi from coming for her again. It was this knowledge that troubled Sebastian's dreams.

* * *

Michaela did not wake until the sunlight inched across the unfamiliar moss-green comforter draped over her torso. The light changed the deep hue to a leaf-green color and reminded her of the mixed sunlight through a forest canopy. She blinked at the ceiling, feeling relaxed and more rested than she had felt in weeks.

Where was she?

She gave a tentative stretch, feeling sore in unexpected places, as she came up against something warm and solid. Michaela felt an inward groan as details surfaced like corks released underwater. Each one bobbed up, bringing a new disturbance to the clear pool her thoughts had been.

Sebastian.

Her eyes widened as she recalled his touch, his kiss and then their… Oh, God. She sunk farther into the mattress. What in the name of heaven had possessed her? The man traveled through the sky and would not tell her all of what was happening. Yet when he touched her, kissed her, sweet Lord above, who kissed like that? He had done things to her, anticipated her desires in a way that now caused the small hairs on her neck to prickle a warning.

She inched away and felt his grip on her arm tighten. A glance told her he still slept, innocently with his mouth open slightly and his breathing relaxed and regular. Yet even in his slumber he imprisoned her.

She stared at his tousled hair and handsome face. No wonder she was attracted to him; any woman would be. The man's rugged features gave him a striking masculine beauty that made it hard for her to breathe. She resisted the urge to stroke his smooth cheek and the sculpted jaw, knowing something was amiss. What was it?

And then she realized. He had slept beside her through the night, the entire night, and yet his face looked as if he had just shaved. Where was the stubble that should darken his chin?

She inched still farther away. He had protected her from Nagi, but who would protect her from him?

His grip tightened and his eyes snapped open. They stared at each other in silence for a moment as his gaze roamed over her face, as if he searched it for answers to her sudden withdrawal. Could he feel her heart pounding?

"Why would you need protection from me?" he asked, and then his eyes shifted away as if he considered several possibilities.

It was at that moment that she remembered something, something he had said. He could read her mind when he touched her. Her eyes widened as everything snapped into clear focus. His masterful touch, his perfect timing—their lovemaking. He had used her in a way that made her flush in shame.

She snatched back her arm, but he did not release her.

"Let go of me," she ordered.

He hesitated, looking at his hand forming the connection between them. His grip was punishing now, bruising her skin, but before she could grimace, his fingers slipped away.

She scrambled off the bed, recalling too late that she was naked. She snatched the comforter, holding the bulky cover before her, now tethered to the bed.

She would have to release it to flee. He stared at her, waiting, eyes watchful. She threw down the corner of the covering and marched to the bathroom, feeling his gaze measure her every step.

She found her old jeans where she had left them and drew them up with angry yanks over her bare hips. She retrieved her top and sleeveless shirt, loathe to pull them on, but needing the modesty they provided. Only then did she notice the huge fur rug lying in a heap on the floor. She stooped to stroke the thick hair and wondered where it came from. She was still frowning in confusion when he entered the room. Michaela glanced up, her breath catching at his magnificent bare chest. He scooped up the hide and held it in one hand. By accident or design, it covered the most distracting part of him, which allowed Michaela's brain to reengage.

"Michaela, listen…"

She did, but he said nothing further. It seemed that without the help of his mind link, he was at a loss to read her. But last night…

She straightened to face him. "No wonder! You were reading my mind, weren't you?"

"Yes." Sebastian eyed her with the same caution he had used the day he had accidentally cornered a wolverine. She looked just as trapped and just as dangerous.

"And that's why you knew, to kiss me here." She motioned to her neck, and then her hand clamped over her mouth and her face brightened to a compelling pink that reminded him of the flush of her skin.

"It was what you wanted."

She pointed an accusatory finger at him. "You

cheated. I never would have let you do that, but you were so perfect as if…not as if, you did know—everything!" The rising tenor of her voice made it sound as if he had tricked her, instead of doing everything she desired.

"I don't understand. I gave you pleasure." He reached for her, seeking the bond that would reveal her thoughts.

She slapped at his hand and backed away. "Don't touch me."

"I only did what you willed me to do."

"Willed you? I don't even know what the hell you are and I let you…" She pressed both hands over her mouth again, then slid them up to cradle her forehead, snaking her fingers through the dark tangles of her hair.

His frustration got the better of him. Without the contact he could make no sense of her ravings. He considered grabbing her, but feared that this might make him want her again. He did, even without the contact and even knowing she was unwilling. The desire he felt before was now magnified by the knowledge of the perfection of their joining.

The female grizzlies he had known were not like this. They wanted one thing and were insistent, and like Michaela, they had no use for him after the deed was done. If he overstayed his welcome, the female would take a swing at him. Of course, male grizzlies had a bad habit of eating the young, so it was natural to chase him off after he served his purpose. And he was of no use in that respect, being infertile except—his eyes met hers as the realization struck him…except with humans. The dread was sharp and brief.

But she could not conceive by him because she did

not love him. Instead of the sweeping relief he expected, he felt the sharp jabbing point of regret. He didn't want offspring, not when he knew what they would be forced to become. But to have the love of such a woman, that would be so sweet.

Michaela had her arms tight over her chest now. The gesture only pushed her breasts more closely together so they swelled invitingly over the pink top. His pulse raced as lust hit him with gripping force. He pressed his hide over his rising erection.

"I only did what any male would have done." And what he wanted to do again.

"Any male?" Her voice held acid. "Any male? What the hell is that? You ride on tornadoes and heal people with eagle feathers. Don't tell me you are just like any of my old boyfriends."

"You regret this joining?" He began to feel the same, but doubted her concerns were similar to his.

"Regret? Oh, we're way past that."

He glanced into her eyes, trying to find some sign to follow, and saw only the twin tracks of her tears. This development rattled him far worse than anything he'd faced before.

With no guidance from Michaela, he fell back to what his instinct told him to do when faced with a threat—attack or run.

She swiped angrily at her tears, pressing her trembling lips together in an obvious fight for control. He admired her for the struggle and paused, captivated by her internal battle with her emotions. It was so easy to become lost in those soulful, troubled eyes.

Chapter 10

Michaela dashed the hot tears from her face and held her breath a moment. She would not bawl like a baby. She would not.

This was her fault as much as his. Though it galled her to admit, even to herself, that he *had* only accepted what she had offered.

He could read her thoughts.

It was like being robbed without knowing anything was missing. He tried again to touch her and she lifted a hand to stay him.

"No."

He lowered his chin as if preparing to fight. She could see from his sullen expression that he was used to getting his way. Well, not this time!

He peered at her from beneath his thick brow. "You couldn't best me."

"But I will make it as difficult for you as possible."

His mouth quirked. "Submission is your only option. You are outmatched and cornered."

"As with Nagi, it won't stop me from fighting."

That took some of the wind from his sails, for his advance faltered. It seemed he didn't like being compared to her tormentor.

It was a cheap shot, but hey, she wasn't going to outmuscle him. Wits were all she had. Unfortunately she had not used them last night.

"Listen, Buster." She tried her best no-nonsense voice as she struggled to ignore the miles of tempting naked flesh before her. "You can't just creep into my mind uninvited."

"You did invite me last night."

"Things look clearer in the morning."

Michaela's body hummed at his proximity as she felt the heat of his body, but she held tight to her fury. It protected her from the hunger his gaze roused within her. If he touched her, he'd know the truth, that despite her wrath, she still wanted him.

He had done things to her last night, wonderful, masterful things. But now she understood how he did them. He stole the information, right out of her mind.

"Put on some clothes, Romeo."

He glanced down as if just noticing their absence, then strode unabashedly down the hall, giving her a spectacular view of the workings of the male anatomy, specifically the corded muscles along his spine and his tight ass.

He returned a moment later wearing cargo pants slung low on his hips. They looked ready to slide off at any moment and weren't thick enough to disguise his stellar erection. She gulped and looked away as the tingle of desire stirred her, making her slick and ready.

He leaned against the doorjamb, regarding her as if she were the most puzzling creature he had ever met.

There was so much about this that she did not understand. She didn't expect him to trust her. If she had some big honking secret, she wouldn't tell him, either. But then she didn't have to, because he could steal her secrets right out of her head.

"Can you see everything, or only what I'm thinking?"

"Thinking." His smile was sensual as all hell. "Feeling."

She tried not to think back, but despite her efforts, her mind rolled back to the intensity of her orgasm. She met his gaze. "Feeling?"

His self-satisfied smile told her he was recalling the same thing.

"Oh, yeah."

She flapped her arms in frustration. "Why did you sleep with me?"

He lost his smile and his brow wrinkled. "Because I was not strong enough to resist what you offered."

That cut her. She folded her arms across her chest as if her crossed arms could protect her from his harsh words. It was almost as if she stood naked before him again, only this time she did not feel cherished, but exposed and ashamed. Her pulse pounded in her throat and face.

"God's gift, are you?"

"I know I pleased you."

She couldn't even deny it for he knew. "Geesh. That's some ego you got there, Adonis. You expect me to jump every time you crook your finger?"

He shook his head in confusion. "If you enjoy our coupling—why not?"

Coupling—as if they were freight cars. His choice of words added fuel to the fire.

"Because I'm not your sex toy."

He understood that reference, thanks to Nicholas and a very odd magazine his friend had bought him as a joke. His friend said he needed to come out of the woods. Sebastian had used the paper to start a fire to cook some graylings.

"All right," he conceded. "You are the female. So you tell me when you want to mate."

Her jaw dropped. Obviously, he had said something wrong again because her eyes threw daggers at him.

"When hell freezes over." She lifted her chin and looked away in a show of displeasure.

His eyes narrowed. He took a step in her direction and then another, soundlessly as any good predator would, but she caught the movement and retreated until the back of her legs hit the counter, forcing her to make her stand. He lifted a hand, but she struck it away.

He hesitated.

"A long time, then?" he asked as if taking a stab.

She lifted her gaze to meet his, seeing that he did not understand her any better than she did him. It stole all her outrage, transforming it into melancholy. "Pleasure is not all that comes from lovemaking."

His brow wrinkled.

When she spoke again, her voice came in a humiliated whisper. "I could get pregnant."

"No, rabbit. You could not."

He sounded rock-sure. Little needles of uncertainty prickled her neck.

"How do you know?"

"Do you love me?" he asked.

"What?"

"Answer the question."

"I want to punch you in the face."

He smiled a sad little smile. "Then I can't impregnate you."

"Vasectomy?"

He winced. "No. I can only sire offspring with a woman who loves me and whom I love. Wanting to punch me doesn't qualify."

"You get that from the book about storks?"

"Storks?"

"It's bullshit."

"No, it's not."

She almost believed him, did believe him enough to have doubts. She stared a moment too long at his curving mouth and felt the touchdown of another tornado of longing.

"Sometimes I don't have to touch you to know what you are thinking," he whispered.

She dropped her gaze to her toes. He'd caught her ogling him only moments after telling him to keep his distance. She was acting like a schizophrenic. This time, when she spoke, it was from the heart.

"I don't understand what is happening. I just want to go home."

He could not explain why the pain in her voice cut through him like a weapon. But it did. "You cannot go home because the Spirit Wound is not healing."

She gave her shoulder a tentative shrug. It did nothing more than answer with a dull ache. "It doesn't feel so bad."

He reached and she evaded.

She met his frustrated gaze.

"It *is* bad, Michaela. You know this."

She set her jaw in stubborn refusal to concede the truth.

"I must take you north."

"When?" she demanded.

"When you have more strength."

"I had enough strength for you to sleep with me."

She watched that poisoned arrow hit home. He frowned and scratched his neck at the hairline.

"We will go tomorrow."

"Why wait?" She folded her arms in challenge.

He stared at her, letting his gaze travel from head to toe.

"You sure about the babies?" she asked, her voice losing its bravado.

He nodded.

She shook her head in confusion.

A large bird flew by the window, dipping a wing and calling. Sebastian's attention shifted to the black shadow until it disappeared from sight, and then he glanced back at Michaela.

"Do not leave the lodge."

The muscles around her mouth grew tight.

He pointed a finger at her to make certain she understood. "You must stay here."

And then he strode from the room and out of the lodge without a backward glance.

Michaela stood on the deck facing the lake. She had hastily drawn on her hiking boots as she scanned the sky for the raven that she was certain triggered Sebastian's hasty withdrawal.

Her attention moved methodically over her surroundings. On the lake a pair of loons swam low in the water, their beaks lifted as if in disdain. Along the shore a blue heron walked with practiced stillness, his sharp yellow eyes scanning the water for breakfast. The world looked at perfect peace.

Staring out at the calm of the morning, she could hardly believe everything seemed so normal. But like the glassy surface of the lake, it was an illusion. Below the surface, out of sight, monsters prowled.

She felt she was being watched and glanced around, finding the raven eyeing her from atop the tallest pine. They stared at each other for a moment, before it stretched its wings and glided silently through the trees and out of sight.

She had not seen Sebastian, who had vanished like the wind on which he traveled. But she felt certain if she just followed that damned bird, she'd come upon him. Michaela descended the stairs, pausing at the last step as she recalled Sebastian's orders. Were they spoken to protect her or his secrets?

She wanted answers and that meant finding what he was up to.

Michaela set her jaw and stepped off the bottom stair, traveling along the lakeshore in the direction the bird had gone.

She shortly found a trail, evident in the dewy grass.

She scrambled over a fallen tree and paused a moment to lean against the sturdy trunk. From the corner of her vision she saw movement. She turned, half expecting to see the raven flitting through the branches, but that was not what caught her eye. Something like a wisp of smoke from burning leaves hovered, there by the tree line! She stared at the spot but now saw nothing. Fog? She hurried on, suddenly rattled by her unfamiliar surroundings.

Her imagination, she decided, all this talk of ghosts.

It made no sense that Nagi should want her. She hadn't killed anyone or done any great evil. Until yesterday, she had believed that Nagi was just a means to frighten children into behaving themselves, the Sioux version of karmic justice.

Now she entertained terrible possibilities. She actually wondered what the heck Nagi, warden for all bad ghosts, was doing in this circle? She paused, recognizing that she believed it—all of it.

Her skin tingled a warning. Was he pursuing her even now? It accounted for the creeping sensation and the smoke.

She glanced down the shoreline, surprised at how far she had walked from the lodge. Something wasn't right. Every nerve in her body screamed a warning. She turned back, suddenly anxious to reach the safety of the deck.

Sebastian's warning replayed in her mind. *Don't leave the lodge.*

Why would he trick her?

Her heart pounded as she stood perfectly still. The calm now seemed ominous rather than peaceful, like the anxious lull before battle.

He had told her something else, back at his home. Ghosts could not reach her there. The structure was protected by some means, and she had left it to go on some half-cocked spy mission.

When she came to the largest of the fallen logs, she slowed to throw her leg up and over, but before it touched down on the other side, she heard the ominous rattle.

She had never heard a rattlesnake before, but she recognized it instantly. The papery shudder, like dried beans shaken in a paper bag, was unmistakable. She froze with one foot on the ground and one across the log as she scanned the ground beneath her. It was there, coiled to strike with its wide, flat head raised, a huge snake, with a body as thick as a vacuum hose. She stared at the flicking red tongue and the unnatural yellow eyes.

Chapter 11

The reeds lashed Sebastian's legs, soaking his trousers as he made his way along the shoreline. The rocks scraped the unprotected skin of his feet and so he transformed before continuing at a lope.

When he had come a half mile, he sat on a mossy patch of rock to wait. Better that he let her find him.

Sebastian barely noted the rustle of wings as the large raven alighted on the stump not five feet away. She regarded him with her bead-black eyes and then spoke.

"I understand you have a visitor." Her voice was strange and crackling, like a myna bird's. Bess had the power to speak while still in animal form.

He raised his head, calling for the power to change, enduring the familiar electric buzz that rippled through him as he transformed back into a man. "Hello, Bess."

The feathers on her head lifted. "Nicholas is behind me, but some miles back. He said you witnessed a human attacked by Nagi."

Sebastian nodded, suddenly feeling tired.

"I've never heard of such a thing. Why is he in this plane?"

"I don't know."

"Does she have some special gifts that might appeal to him?"

Sebastian had thought of that. "She can see Spirits when she is awake."

Bess flapped her wings in surprise, causing her to lift an inch from the stump. "Really?" She landed and folded back her wings, wiggling to adjust them. "Nicholas said to tell you that he could not find her parents."

Sebastian nodded. If Nicholas could not find them, they were both dead. He brooded a moment.

Bess transformed so she was now sitting on the stump. Her long black hair was drawn into an impossibly long braid that was as thick as the body of a weasel and just as glossy. Her winged brows swept over her dark eyes in a troubled expression as she leaned toward him, making her billowing black blouse gape in the front to reveal impressive cleavage.

"Why did you interfere, brother? Humans are not our affair."

"We're half human, Bess."

She stood. Bess was a surprisingly tall woman, but thin and fine-boned, making her look like a dancer. Her fanciful skirt only added to her grace as she swept forward.

He told Bess of Nagi's failed attempt to possess him

and of his choice to take Michaela in rather than leave her to die. He explained his limited success at drawing the poisons from her wound. Finally, he told her of his plan to take her to Kanka.

Bess nodded her agreement to this. "Kanka has the power to heal this wound *if* she chooses to help a human. Likely she will also know why Nagi wants this one. Whether she will consent to tell you is another matter."

"Michaela has some power," he offered. "Perhaps she's not human."

She swept an index finger over the hair at her temple as if preening. "Perhaps she *is* a human who got knocked on the head, died and then somehow escaped from the Circle of Ghosts."

"No one escapes the Circle. You know it."

"I know only that no one ever has." Bess cocked her head, keeping her bright eye on him. "But if that is where she belongs, Nagi is entitled to have her back."

"No."

"No, because it is not so, or no, because you do not wish it to be so?"

"She is not evil. If her soul was black, I would know."

"How?"

He shifted uncomfortably. "I sense her thoughts."

Bess's dark brow lifted over her startled eyes. It was an expression he had not seen for she was so rarely surprised.

Now her brow swept low over her dark eyes, making her look fierce. "Are you the only one who can sense her thoughts?"

"I do not know."

"I would like to meet her."

"No."

Bess's sharp eyes turned knowing. "You care for her, this little one."

"I do not."

"Yet you shelter her, even from me."

It was true. Michaela made him feel more defensive than he had ever felt about anyone or anything. Some of the fight drained out of him. "I don't understand it."

Bess's smile turned sympathetic. "Then, don't try. Just follow your instincts. They are true, even when your mind is divided. But, Sebastian, you cannot tell her you are Inanoka. I never even told Gordon."

"Gordon was a raven."

"And smarter than most people I know."

He held his tongue. Bess still missed her mate; he could see it in the tightening of her mouth and the defiant lifting of her chin. She was ready to defend him even after death. Sebastian suppressed a twinge of jealousy.

He respected that kind of pair bond, envied her that.

"What do you know of her people?" asked Bess.

"I once saw her mother. Human, I think, and followed the ancient ways." He told Bess where she lived. "All I know of her father will come from you."

"Ah," she said. "You are sure the mother was human?"

"Fairly."

"Then, if the woman has special abilities, they came from her sire. Do you have his name?"

"Michael Proud."

"I will fly to the Spirit Road and call his name. I might be able to find him."

Only Inanoka of the Raven Clan had the power to

cross the Way of Souls and return. Her other gift was meddling in everyone's business. But for once he was grateful. He would take any help he could get.

Bess cocked her head, listening. "Is she safe?"

"Yes. I ordered her to stay at my home."

Bess's expression registered alarm.

Sebastian now heard the sound of something clumsily making its way along the lake trail, snapping branches and rustling leaves as loudly as a buffalo. "Damn it!"

Sebastian set off at a dead run. Behind him, Bess lifted into the air, flying straight up to the top of an oak above them.

Michaela stared unblinkingly at the coiled serpent.

So this was the ghost, possessing a creature, using it for its purpose. It would not retreat and it did not matter what she did. It would attack and she knew she could not move fast enough to escape before it sank its poisonous fangs into her exposed calf.

No, this was no longer just a snake. It was a ghost, a ghost that had once been a man. Not Nagi. She knew that, but she did not know how. This had been a man, had been…oh, no, a rapist who had attacked many women and had beaten his wife with… It came to her in flashing pictures, like a slide show. He had used the base of a brass lamp, still connected to the wall, to crush her cheekbones and flatten her nose to raw meat. And he had enjoyed it. He'd gone to jail for a time, but he had no regrets. He enjoyed the violence, relished the power. It was why it had not yet struck. The thing waited merely to increase her terror, savoring her panic, toying with her, all the while knowing she could not move fast enough to escape him. Yes, this soul belonged in the Circle of Ghosts.

But Nagi had sent him instead to hunt her.

She could feel his anticipation and his anxiousness to taste her. He congratulated himself with smug satisfaction for his control at not taking what he wanted until he had squeezed all he could from her anguish. This thing thrived on fear and she gave it exactly what it craved.

His head drew back, lifting farther from the coiled, muscular body. She braced for the strike and the pain that would follow as she stumbled backward off the log.

Chapter 12

A tremendous crash preceded the grizzly's emergence onto the path. The snake turned to face this threat and struck with such speed that Michaela saw only a blur and the slashing of a great paw. One of the bear's claws hooked into the snake's pale underbelly, gutting it with a single stroke. The snake writhed as it sailed through the air. Black smoke billowed from the wound. Was she seeing a ghost?

She lost her footing, fell and then scrambled to her feet, running from the bear and into the lake. Her legs bogged down and she dove, fearing the creature would follow, knowing bears had no fear of water. When she surfaced, she saw a raven grip the inert carcass of the snake in its claws as it rose to the treetops. The bear stood on the shore, its attention focused on her for a moment, and then returned the way it had come.

Sebastian had sent them. She was certain.

"Thank you," she called.

At her words, the bear paused and glanced back at her before disappearing into the woods.

She could not keep a shiver from dancing up her spine. She recognized that bear, had seen it when Nagi had first attacked her. But they were miles from that place now, weren't they?

Honestly, she didn't know exactly where she was. Somehow she had fallen through Alice's looking glass into a world that seemed familiar, but was not. The rules she had followed all her life were now turned upside down and she was lost.

Suddenly sleeping with Sebastian seemed like the least of her worries. Whatever he was, he had acted to defend her. But it was difficult to trust a man knowing that he might pull up stakes at any time and pull the same disappearing act as her father. After that, how could she count on any man to be there when she needed him?

As if summoned by her thoughts, Sebastian loped up the shore wearing his low-riding green cargo pants, high fringed moccasins and nothing to cover his magnificent chest. Sunlight danced across his golden skin, showing the contraction and relaxation of his muscular bulk. His expression was concerned, but not frightened, as his gaze stayed focused on her.

The flood of relief buckled her knees, dunking her again in the icy water. She surfaced, sputtering, and waded out of the lake. She had never been happier to see anyone in her entire life. Michaela ran the last few steps to meet him and threw herself into his arms. She pressed her cheek to his warm chest and squeezed her eyes shut against the nightmare of the past few minutes.

His arms came around her, cradling her tenderly. Tears welled in her eyes as he stroked her hair, hushing her as she cried.

"Thank you for sending them."

He said nothing.

She leaned back to gaze up at him. "The raven and the bear, you sent them. Didn't you?"

His eyes evaded hers. "You left the lodge."

"I'm sorry."

He drew her away and gazed down at her, cocking his head, and she knew he saw her thoughts.

"Trust," he murmured. "You didn't trust." His eyes rounded. "I'm not your father. I won't abandon you."

She gaped at him. She hadn't been thinking that—had she? But then where did he pull that from?

Her head drooped and she sagged against him.

"You're safe now."

"But for how long?"

He did not answer, and she felt her security slip away like sand through a sieve. She broke the embrace.

Motion caught her eye. The raven drifted through the trees, now holding the snake in its shiny black beak. The bird landed on a branch above them and ruffled its feathers.

"How did you know about the snake?" she asked.

The raven shook the grisly trophy. A familiar rattle issued from the dead snake.

"I heard you on the trail." He glanced at the raven, which seemed to give an almost imperceptible nod.

Michaela shielded her eyes and turned her attention to the velvety black bird. "I've never seen one this close. It's beautiful."

The raven ruffled its feathers and an instant later settled them in perfect order, then it draped the snake over the branch on which it perched. It rested a claw over the treasure. The bird turned its glossy head as if eavesdropping.

Sebastian eyed the rattler. "No business being this far north."

She gazed at the ruined body. "It had business with me."

His troubled eyes met hers. "Yes."

She kept her eyes on the grim sight as she spoke. "He'll send more ghosts."

Sebastian's brow descended low over his eyes as he stared at her. "That was a ghost?"

"Possessed by one."

"How do you know?"

"I saw the shadowy thing leave the snake when it died."

"Saw it?" The disbelief rang clear in his voice.

"And heard its thoughts. This ghost was evil. He attacked women, enjoyed attacking them."

The raven chortled as if discontent, its head feathers lifting straight up.

His eyes never left Michaela. "No one can hear ghosts."

"But I did, or sensed it. I don't think I heard it exactly, but I knew what it was feeling and thinking. He raped women, eleven women. The youngest was nineteen and the oldest…" She squeezed her eyes shut as the truth came to her. "The oldest was sixty-six. He kept the newspaper clipping in a green scrapbook with the image of a bouquet of violets on the cover."

Sebastian scowled.

Desperate for reassurance, she forged on. "But you can see them—the ghosts?"

If Sebastian saw them, it would be all right for her to see them. But his expression told her that he did not and that she was as unnatural as a two-headed calf.

He cast out a troubled breath. "I smell them and I can see those eyes when they take possession of a living thing, but I cannot hear their thoughts, nor can I see them when they have no body."

How was it she had a power that he lacked?

"But you hear them?" She waited, her stomach aching at the silence that she filled by rushing ahead. "I could hear him, in my mind. He wanted to bite me. It had been so long since he attacked a woman. He…he used to…to…" She could not put the dreadful images into words and so clamped her hands to her temples as if to cast them out.

Sebastian could not bear to witness her struggle. He laid a hand upon the bare back of her neck, taking her thoughts into his mind. Instead of struggling for her freedom, she grasped his forearm, strengthening the contact, as if she needed him to perceive what haunted her. He swayed at the ugly images. These thoughts were not hers but she *had* seen them and felt the raw emotions. How was this possible?

"You *did* hear it." He stared in wonder.

"I never did before." Her voice held dull resignation, as if adding a burden to one who already had more than she could carry. "Maybe the wound did something to me—triggered it?"

"No, Michaela. A touch from the Spirit World cannot give you such powers. It could only magnify the powers you already possess."

She trembled now as uncertainty blossomed into fear. "I don't have powers."

"You do. You hear ghosts. You *see* ghosts. This alone would be reason enough for Nagi to pursue you."

"I thought his job was to keep the bad ghosts away from the human world, not unleash them on women."

"Who taught you this?"

Her chin sank to her chest, and a wave of sorrow coursed through her so strongly Sebastian was tempted to let go of her to avoid suffering this sorrow with her.

"My mother."

Her mother who had died recently and Michaela had lost the one person in the world who loved her unconditionally. Sebastian sighed in resignation, stemming his rising envy. She'd had a mother who had cared for her.

He had met her mother, after a fashion, had seen her watching him on the rare occasion that he crossed the line of spruce and into the world of man. She had a dreamcatcher on her porch and he heard her chanting prayers at sunrise. This woman followed the old ways.

"She taught you well," he said. "Nagi *is* charged with keeping order in the Circle of Ghosts. It is his domain. But some ghosts do not take the Spirit Road at death, choosing to linger in places they feel most familiar. He collects the bad ones. Have you seen these ghosts before?"

She was thinking hard, recalling vague dreads,

jangling internal bells, warning her to keep clear of a certain room or told her not to venture down a particular street. Were those feelings somehow connected to ghosts?

"I've never heard their thoughts exactly or seen them directly before."

Sebastian slid his hand up to circle the thin column of her neck, finding her thoughts clearer when unveiled by the sodden fabric separating them. "But you are aware of their presence in this plane, have been conscious of them for some time."

"Yes."

"Have you ever read the thoughts of Nagi?"

"No. But he spoke to me in my mother's cabin as I told you."

Sebastian tensed. "What were his words exactly?"

"He said, 'I see you.'"

The raven cawed its warning call in one short burst.

Sebastian glanced up for just an instant before returning his gaze to Michaela. "Could it be that he could not see you before?"

She shrugged. "You tell me. I'm way out of my league here."

"What has changed for you recently?"

More flashes, like summer lightning in a violent storm. Her mother's death, the accident, pain, spinning sensations, and her body not responding to her mind's call, a long stretch of darkness and then grief.

"Darkness?" he asked.

She looked at him with resignation. "Can't you read that? Reception fuzzy? Maybe you can check the cable feed."

"Your thoughts are clearer than your words at times." He pressed his hand to the flesh exposed at her throat, trying to ignore the enticing pulse of her beating heart and the warm flush that blossomed across her chest. "Be still now and think about the accident."

She did, and he read the moments before the mountain bike crashed, the tumbling and the breaking of bones as she fell into the rocks. Her leg and thigh. Sebastian swept a finger over the bump where her collarbone had knit.

She kept her eyes on him, recalling awakening freezing cold, stretched out beneath a white sheet in a thin gown of cotton. He felt the tube in her nose and the one thrust into her bladder. Two needles pierced her hand and forearm. The suspended bags of fluid dripped into the tube forced into her arm. Beside her, machines bleating incessantly, like lambs at shearing. He recalled with her, her terror at finding herself in this metal bed and then the panic at the blank places of her memory.

Hospitals. The barbarism of these places still astonished him. Here they cut away damaged flesh, removing it like a brown spot from an apple.

"What was it?" he asked.

"Coma."

Sebastian growled. "You said only that you were in intensive care."

"I was, but I was unconscious for five days."

"Just unconscious?"

Her answer came into his mind. *I died, twice.*

"Died?" he asked.

"My heart stopped in the ambulance and again in the E.R. Not for very long. No brain damage, they said."

"You opened a portal to the Spirit World. You visited and returned. That is why Nagi can see you now."

The raven gave a low chortle.

Sebastian walked Michaela back to the lodge and up the steps where Bess, still in raven form, kept watch from the peak of the roof.

"If you can see ghosts, you would be of interest to Nagi. But why try to kill you?" he asked.

Michaela's sodden boots dragged and water dripped from her jeans and squished in her socks. Her rounded shoulders and tired step made her look defeated.

"I just want it to stop."

"That may not be possible. You have powers, but you are not like me."

"And what are you, exactly?" She slipped from his grasp and the gloom of her mood vanished from his mind.

He pressed his lips together and he hesitated, wishing he could tell her. She had already seen Nagi and now a ghost.

"You can control animals, ride tornadoes, heal wounds. That makes you like an über-shaman."

"I am not a shaman.

"So…what the heck are you?" She scowled. "'Cause you're not human."

"Says who?"

"Well, you keep calling me human, so I figure that means you'd check 'other' in the species box."

"My mother was human."

"That's less reassuring than you might imagine."

The raven lighted on the porch rail, the feathers at her cowl lifted in agitation as she bobbed her head.

Sebastian scowled at Bess, wishing she'd go away.

Michaela's voice lowered to a reverent whisper. "Does she understand you?"

Sebastian glowered at the bird. "I've never thought so."

Bess began cawing, chewing him a new one as she flapped her wings. Her tirade made conversation difficult.

Michaela cooed at the bird. "You're beautiful and so brave."

Bess's feathers settled as she turned a beady eye on Michaela. Flattery was something that Bess responded to, but when he tried it, she always saw right through him. Michaela's genuine praise must have made the difference.

"Is she a pet?" she asked, raising her hand to stroke the glossy feathers.

Sebastian laughed. Michaela gaped at him, suddenly dumbstruck. She acted as if she'd never heard him laugh.

He stopped, realizing that she hadn't heard him. He never laughed, until now. He felt a squeezing pressure in his chest that might have been joy. It felt wonderful and terrible all at once.

Michaela realized she stood with her hand raised before the great bird. She studied the long beak, noting the wicked-looking hooked tip, and dropped her hand.

"Wise," said Sebastian.

The raven jumped off the rail, stretching its great wings as it flew across the lake and out of sight.

"Serves her right for eavesdropping."

Michaela watched until she lost the bird against the far shore, then turned back to him. "What?"

He stared off in the direction the bird had taken, then pressed a hand to the small of Michaela's back and ushered her inside.

She liked the reassurance of his touch, it made her feel safe. His skin grew hot as his blood pulsed to the most obvious of places. Was it to be like this every time he came within sight of her?

"How did you know to send the grizzly after the possessed bear?"

"I can smell ghosts when they've taken possession."

"What? Really?"

He nodded, stepping closer, wanting to breathe in her warm honey scent and feel her soft skin.

"What do they smell like?"

"Death."

Her eyes rounded.

"Putrid flesh stinking of rot, disease and earth. I can smell them three hundred yards away."

"How is that possible?"

"How is it possible for you to see them?"

She was dripping wet from her jump in the lake, so he took her to the bathroom, pulling a towel from the rack and using it to dry her hair.

He wondered if it were too much to hope that Bess would go away.

"They look like greasy smoke and their eyes glow a sickly yellow." She looked up at him with wide, frightened eyes. "I think I'm going crazy."

"You're changing."

Her eyes were on him once more, full of hopelessness and fear. "Into what?"

"We shall see in time."

Tears rose in her eyes, filling them until the lower lids seemed barely able to contain the rising water. The need to protect her built within him, making him feel he must guard her even from herself.

He reached for her, capturing her round the waist and drawing her into his embrace. She wrapped her arms around his neck and rested her damp head upon his chest.

"Please tell me what's happening to me," she begged.

Hot tears splashed against his bare skin as he stroked her hair, absorbing the torment of her bewilderment and dread.

"I do not know, little one."

She sniffed, and he rocked her until her breathing returned to a steady pace and water no longer flowed from her eyes. Her tears reminded him of his mother.

He released her, then stepped toward the door.

"Where are you going?" she called.

"To get you some dry clothes."

"But you said you don't have any."

He stopped to glance back at her and then left the room, removing his calf-high moccasins. He had never done this before, never given a piece of himself to someone. If the garment were lost he'd have a fist-size hole in his coat as a reminder of his foolishness.

He held out one moccasin and shook it, changing the leather into green silk the same color as her eyes. It was a slinky dress he'd seen on a calendar in a bookstore. The image had stuck and so he was able to re-create it. He held the garment by the shoulders, wondering if it would fit.

Finally, he changed his remaining knee-high footwear into a pair of running shoes, then returned to her.

He extended his gift. “Here.”

She accepted the dress with openmouthed wonder, holding it out to examine it.

“Lovely.” She lowered the silk and stared at him, a smile on her face. “Why in the world would you have something like this here?”

“I didn’t until a minute ago.”

Her playful expression vanished, replaced by the lost look. He hated that he had robbed her of the little moment of joy.

“Put it on. I’m expecting company.”

Chapter 13

Michaela looked out through the French doors at the tall woman on the porch. Her black hair was swept up in a sculptural bun, emphasizing her statuesque features and elegant form. She was draped to the knee in a stylish flowing black dress that reminded Michaela of something made for movement. The garment that flowed about her looked like the wings of a bird or a ballerina taking the stage.

The Black Swan—that was what she looked like. Michaela thought her wardrobe out of place in such a locale, until she glanced down at her own sleek cocktail dress. She peered toward the kitchen and saw Sebastian arranging three cups on the counter, but making no attempt whatsoever to answer the door.

So Michaela greeted their guest, who swept in as if completely comfortable in this place.

"Hello." She smiled and extended her hand. "I'm Bess."

Michaela stared for a moment at the long, elegant fingers and sculpted nails, devoid of any polish but carefully tended. They clasped hands.

"Michaela Proud."

"Enchanted." Bess did not release her hand, but kept possession as if waiting for something to happen.

Michaela resisted the urge to tug free as Bess scrutinized her.

At last the woman freed her hand but still held contact with her eyes. Disquieted by the odd sense of familiarity in her inquisitive stare, Michaela dropped her gaze and noted Bess's lovely necklace. Black crystal beads circled her graceful neck. At the base of her throat hung a carving of a black bird with a red jewel in its open beak. She'd never seen a fetish like this one. The details of the wings were magnificent, and she recognized the symbolism immediately—Raven stealing the sun.

"What a lovely dress," said Bess.

"Oh." Michaela ran her fingers over the silk sleeve. "My clothing's wet. Sebastian gave it to me."

Bess's dark brow lifted as she glanced at her host, but said nothing. "Hello, Sebastian."

He nodded a greeting. "Tea?"

He drew out a cookie tin that once held Danish butter cookies, and opened it.

Michaela perched on a stool at the counter as Sebastian lined up a bag of sugar, a bottle of molasses, a jar of honey and a bag of brown sugar before offering them a spoon and cup.

"Thank you."

He poured and she tore open the envelope, plopping the tea bag into her mug as Michaela tried to reconcile the normalcy of the scene with the unsettling oddities.

"I didn't see another cabin nearby," said Michaela.

"Oh, mine is tucked way up in those tall pines behind this place."

"I see," Michaela said, not believing a word. Sebastian seemed as solitary as a clam, and it made no sense for them to be neighbors out here, when there was not one other residence visible on the lakeshore. Before she could formulate a question that would not sound rude, Bess asked one of her own.

"How is your injury?"

Michaela could not keep the surprise from her expression. How in the world could this woman know about that? Michaela glanced at the short sleeve of the dress, confirming that no outward indication of the attack was visible. She grew still as the sense of the ordinary dissolved like a sugar cube in tea.

"How did you know?"

"Sebastian mentioned it."

She cast him a glance, but he did not meet her eyes, leaving her alone to face this disconcerting woman.

"Well, it's feeling much better, thanks to..." To what—Sebastian's eagle feather? She settled on "Sebastian's help."

"He's a gem. Although some wounds even he can't mend." Bess cast Sebastian a meaningful glance that made Michaela speculate at the relationship between these two. Her mood turned sour despite the sweetness of her tea.

Not that Michaela had any claim on him. He had made that clear this morning when he'd leaped from her bed as if it were on fire. But that humiliation didn't keep the jealousy from popping up like a gopher in a horse pasture. When he'd taken off like a bullet from a gun, had he run straight to this woman?

Michaela turned her attention back to him and found Sebastian leaning against the counter and watching them both with cautious eyes. His gaze wandered over Michaela, making her flush. When their eyes met, she lowered her gaze to watch the steam rising from the still surface of her tea. Yes, that was exactly how he made her feel.

Bess interrupted her carnal thoughts.

"Sebastian has set me on a little mission." She set her teacup aside and rose.

Sebastian pushed off from his resting place and Michaela trailed them to the door.

Bess paused at the threshold and rested a hand on Michaela's. "Don't travel alone. You have powerful enemies and that calls for powerful friends."

With that she swept through the door.

Sebastian followed her with his eyes, and then met Michaela's. "You'll be all right for a few minutes?"

She nodded, not wanting to tell him how rattled she really felt, not wanting him to see she was a coward.

"You're safe in this house, so stay here this time—promise?"

She nodded and he gave her a smile before following Bess.

Michaela watched them through the glass windows wishing she could read lips.

"She's in real trouble," said Bess. "The damage is spreading."

Now Sebastian's spirits fell. "I checked it this morning. It looked better."

"Because you see only the physical injury, not her aura. Hers is a pretty violet, with a touch of turquoise near her head. I've never seen that combination before. I'm not sure what it means. I can tell you it is unique. But the wound is emitting black energy and it is growing. Soon it will push her aura away from her body. If you don't do something now, she will be lost."

"Dead?"

"I'm not sure, perhaps worse than dead. I'm unfamiliar with this kind of possession."

Bess's powers dealt with the soul, while Sebastian's strengths lay with the body. If she said the danger was growing, he believed her.

"I was waiting until she was stronger to take her to Kanka."

Bess shook her head. "By the time she is physically strong, her soul will be eternally damaged. Sebastian, I know you care for her."

He was about to deny it, and then recalled that Bess could see attraction between souls as clearly as he could smell Michaela's arousal for him. Bess had described it once, an aura that glowed for only one soul. Could Michaela be the one for him?

He longed to ask her, but feared that she might deny any connection. She had not said Michaela cared for him. He squeezed his hands into fists, knowing his relationship with Michaela would end badly; it was inevitable. But he wished, just this once, things could be different.

"I don't want her to die."

Bess's expression turned all doughy with sympathy. For once he was not angered by her show of emotion. Rather, he was grateful for her help.

Bess gripped his hand for just a moment. It was the first time she had ever touched him.

"I have her father's name and I have seen her aura. So I will fly to the Spirit World and call to him."

"Bess, do you actually enter the Spirit World?"

"No one can do that until death. I merely fly to the edge of their territory, the shadow land between dreams and waking. Wandering Spirits answer me. Perhaps one will know of him. I can only try."

"How long will it take to go and return?"

"I never know. Time is funny in the Spirit plane. But I will make haste and I will find you when I return. Go quickly to Kanka."

"Bess, do you think it possible that she is not just human?"

"Many things are possible."

"She's seen the whirlwind and Nagi and other ghosts. Don't you think I could—"

Her smile vanished, replaced by a look of ice. "Stop. Humans do not know of us and that allows us to fulfill our purpose. You are attracted to her. That is not dangerous in itself. We've all had human lovers. But we don't tell them what we are."

Sebastian nodded.

Bess gave him a misty stare. "Be careful, my friend. Their lives are short and this one's is perhaps shorter than most."

"No."

"There are limits even to what we can do."

Sebastian set his jaw in stubborn determination.

Bess sighed. "I see my warnings come too late. I will hurry. Good luck, my friend."

She walked down the stairs and out of the sight of Michaela, watching before the bank of windows. Once well away, Bess stretched her arms wide. Feathers sprouted from her spread fingers as she burst into the air, crying her farewell. He followed her progress with his eyes until she was no more than a black speck upon the blue sky, and then he could not make her out at all.

Bess was right. They must go to Kanka today.

Sebastian paused on the stairs, needing time to think before returning to Michaela.

As he walked away from the house, he thought on Bess's warning. Halflings kept their natures secret. He knew it, and never before had he even considered telling a human. Michaela should be no different.

But somehow she was.

Sebastian kept the house in sight as he walked to the edge of the lake. Why did he even want to tell her?

True, she was the first human to ever show him compassion and the first to cause him to reveal his tender side. And she was brave throughout this ordeal. He admired her courage.

And there was no denying the heat between them. It pulsed with life whenever he got within sight of her. No, he didn't have to see her; just the scent of her aroused him.

But to tell her what he really was would not only jeopardize the anonymity of all Inanoka, no, the danger was greater even than that. For to tell her was to kiss her goodbye. Past experience taught him that revealing his nature would drive her off. He'd made the mistake before and seen the revulsion.

So why did he have this irrational longing to bare his soul to her? He had thought the same once before and been so wrong. That was why he did not understand this stupid, wrongful impression that she was somehow different.

Perhaps she was, but not so different as to accept a Skinwalker in her bed.

Seeing him transform would mark the end for them, and he would be alone once more. He should prefer her confusion about what he was to the certain results a confession would reap. Her speculations did not venture near the truth, for such thoughts were too far outside the realm of her reality for consideration.

To humans, Skinwalkers were folklore. Few of them ever thought to question why such myths pervaded every culture. Silkies, werewolves, Skinwalkers, shapeshifters—each one based in fact.

He picked up a smooth stone and skipped it across the water, then glanced back to the house. Was she watching him through those windows?

He longed to return to her, longed for Michaela to

know his secret. No, that wasn't it exactly. He ached for something more, yearned so deeply he barely dared to bring the thought to consciousness, because to do so was to admit the impossibility of his need and to recognize that what he most wanted. He could never possess and then have to live all the rest of his days without it.

He wanted her to accept him as he was.

How would that feel? He held the sweet possibility for an instant, like sugar dissolving on his tongue.

"No," he growled.

She would never know, because in reaching for that kind of intimacy he risked losing her forever. So, he would take a page from Nicholas's book and enjoy what she offered, while keeping her at arm's length. His world must stay beyond her line of vision.

This was best for them both.

But once he brought her to Kanka, he knew she would have no further use for him. The sense of loss crept through him, like a killing frost. Was that why he delayed? Was his avoidance to do what must be done more about his needs than hers? It shamed him to recognize the truth he had hidden even from himself. He delayed, not for her to grow stronger, but to put off having to let her go. Why he was delaying even now, dawdling out here instead of returning and preparing her for the journey.

He knew that he could not keep Michaela. But he was not ready to give her up.

His thoughts were broken by a distinctive yipping sound that came from the south. Sebastian cocked his head and returned the call with a low growl. A moment later, a gray timber wolf loped into the open, his sides heaving as if he'd run all day.

His long pink tongue lolled as he stretched until his head sank low between his paws in a stately bow. Sebastian nodded in return, recognizing Nicholas's scent. The wolf drew forward, circling Sebastian once. He lifted his head as if to howl and rose into the form of a man.

"How goes it?" asked his friend.

Sebastian formed his question, then hesitated only a moment. Nicholas was less particular about mating and might know something that he did not.

"Can you read their thoughts?"

"Whose thoughts?" asked the wolf.

Sebastian didn't appreciate the phony show of puzzlement. "What do you mean whose? Humans."

"Theirs or just hers?"

"Only hers."

Nicholas glanced at him with an expression that seemed like newfound respect. In addition, all the irreverence had disappeared from his tone. "I have heard of such a connection only between soul mates."

Sebastian was suddenly glad he was sitting down. The hope that swept through him lasted only as long as it takes to smash a glass bottle against a brick wall. He huffed. "That's only a legend."

"Perhaps." Nicholas stroked the skin above his upper lip for a moment as he thought and then glanced back to Sebastian. "Are you sure she is only human, this little one you have found?"

Sebastian snaked his fingers through his hair. "I don't know."

He lifted his nose and inhaled the breeze. Instead of the fresh scent of pine, he noted something else on the wind, the stench of rotting meat and innards bloated and putrid. He glanced skyward, wondering why the buzzards had not found such a ripe carcass.

"Do you smell that?" he asked.

Nicholas glanced behind them. "I do."

When Sebastian realized the stink came from the direction of his lodge, he was on his feet. She hadn't left the house again, not after she had promised him.

His uncertainty forced him into a run.

Chapter 14

Sebastian thundered up the trail, as uncertainty ate him alive.

He saw the empty deck first. Charging on, he spotted her, standing motionless on the very bottom step, her eyes riveted on something in the underbrush. She was safe—wasn't she?

"Michaela," he called.

Her absorption broke at the sound of his voice and she retreated back up the stairway, pointing. He targeted the scent of death, following it to the yellow-eyed coyote. He ran at it in fury, forgetting that she watched. It scrambled clear of his swinging arm, but he struck the young pine beside it, tearing it in half a foot from the base. The coyote tucked its tail and ran into the underbrush, but Sebastian heard it stop at a safe distance. It had not gone far.

He vacillated between continuing to charge and returning to protect Michaela. The pull of the woman won over his wrath and he halted.

Sebastian was halfway up the stairs before he realized that she was retreating from him. Why did she look at him like that, with eyes round and white?

"Michaela?"

He glanced back, checking for threats, and instead saw the ragged stump of the ruined pine. He had attacked the coyote at full speed, moving much faster than a man could run.

Damn, he was not good at concealment. It was one of a hundred reasons he lived alone.

He looked at her, shamed by the fear he now saw reflected on her face.

"Michaela." He reached out. "Are you all right?"

She shook her head in answer. "You broke that tree like a swizzle stick. How—how?"

"I'm stronger than I look." *Change the subject.* "You stayed on the porch."

She nodded, but her eyes pinned him warily as her ears drew back almost imperceptibly. He smelled the fear on the light sheen of sweat now forming on her flushed skin.

She pointed. "There are two now."

He turned around, trying to spot the other coyote.

"In the tree."

He did not see the thing at first, but then homed in on the steady stare of the Cooper's hawk. He would not have known it was possessed.

"Are you certain?"

"She murdered her children. Drowned them in a bathtub. The older one was three days from his second birthday."

It was his turn to stare at her. "She told you that?"

"Her thoughts. She wants to please Nagi. She wants to stay in this world, even as a hawk."

"Preferable to the Circle." He realized now that Nagi could send a hundred ghosts at a time, a thousand.

"We need to get you to Kanka."

"The Sorceress?"

"You know of her?"

"Only from stories my mother told." Her bottom lip trembled. "I never thought she was real, too."

The sight of her about to weep caused his insides to constrict as her pain became his pain. He stepped closer to bring her into the safety of his arms.

But she backed away, her wary eyes upon him. What was she thinking? He needed to touch her to know.

"I'm afraid," she whispered.

He opened his arms to her. "Then let me comfort you."

"No."

"Why?"

"Because I'm afraid of you, most of all."

His arms fell to his sides. Last night she had given herself to him—trusted him in a way he did not know a woman could trust a man. It had been the happiest moment of his life. But now she had seen behind his mask. He was to her what he had been to all humans—a threat.

He straightened. "We must leave this place. Gather up your clothing."

"They're still wet."

"We'll take them." He ushered her inside and stuffed her jeans, shirt, socks, boots and undergarments into a knapsack that he slipped over one shoulder.

Together they left the house, to find a patch of open ground. He turned his attention on Michaela.

"Ready?"

He did not need to touch her to know her mind. Her wide eyes and accelerated breathing showed her rising panic. "I can't breathe past the wind."

"You just are not accustomed to it. You must try."

"Can't we go some other way, something with a layover, maybe?"

He was sorry to disappoint her, even in this. "There is water and we must make haste."

"But in a few days I might be stronger."

"We go now." He wondered if he should tell her the rest. It was her life, after all, but perhaps it was best for her not to know that the wound was now attacking her soul. He wondered how much damage had been wrought already.

He held her in his arms, protecting her from the winds. At the contact he read her turmoil, her desire to escape him and even the flutter of excitement as some small portion of her mind recalled their lovemaking.

He lifted one arm, calling the whirlwind. First came the cry of the Thunderbirds as the dark clouds rolled in from the west.

Sebastian's powerful arms gripped her, and Michaela glanced up for reassurance against her growing terror.

"Take a deep breath now and remember to breathe as we travel. You can do it."

Michaela inhaled deeply as the storm swirled above them. The wind battered her, again trying to tear her from the safety of his arms. But she clung as they rose into the sky, and this time she opened her eyes.

Dark shapes swirled and swooped through the billowing clouds, coming nearer, but still too far for her to make out what they were through the billowing storm. All about them lightning flashed and thunder boomed. Her lungs began to ache until she grew dizzy with the effort of containing the air.

She released her breath only to have it ripped away. She battled to draw another, but she could not.

The air smelled strongly of lightning and was as cold as a January blizzard, freezing her lips and mouth. She trembled in his arms as she wrestled for air, panic seizing her as spots danced before her eyes. Was this the blackness of the storm or her mind losing consciousness?

He tightened his grip, and she looked up to see him trying to speak, but any sound was eaten by the terrible wind. It roared and screamed like a locomotive barreling past her.

She read his lips.

Breathe.

She tried. The cold air frosted her throat but some reached her starved lungs. The wind was too fast, too cold. She was losing herself to the tingling darkness.

Her teeth chattered and her body ached. Gradually, awareness returned. She blinked open her eyes.

Sebastian held her in his arms, staring down with worried eyes.

"Michaela? Have you returned to me?"

She looped her arms around his neck and pressed her face into the warm folds of his heavy fur cloak.

The roaring wind had ceased. Something cold touched her face. She glanced up. It was August, yet a light snow fell. Where were they?

"Have we reached her?" she asked.

"Not yet. I brought us to earth when you went limp. I need to make one more trip of similar length. Are you ready?"

She shook her head, ashamed by her weakness. "I am still dizzy."

He sat with her in the light dusting of snow cradling her beneath his cloak like a child, the heat of his body keeping her warm.

She glanced around, at the tall narrow pines, their thin, spindly forms an indication of the harshness of this place. The clouds hung low, so she could see nothing beyond the silent sentries of black spruce.

"Where are we?"

"Near the Arctic Circle. A wild place in the Brooks Range."

He did not even shiver from the cold, yet he wore only a thin flannel shirt and the hulking brown cloak. She added it to the growing list of things that told how unnatural he was. Whatever he was, he had done nothing but try to protect her. Even without understanding his true nature, she found she trusted him and wished he could trust her. What was the secret that he so feared would turn her from him?

"Give me time, little rabbit. I have lived alone with my secrets so long."

This time she did not scowl at his intrusion into her mind, but only smiled.

"I'm good with secrets."

"All women are good with them, good with sharing them." He stroked her cheek.

For the first time in her life, she felt the urge to put her faith in someone other than herself.

This wasn't her father. This man would not abandon her.

"I will stay as long as you have need of me."

She lifted a hand and stroked his smooth cheek, her gratitude growing with her desire.

He drew back. "You need shelter. This valley has a landing strip and several hunting cabins. We'll go there."

She recalled belatedly that she wore only a thin cocktail dress and running shoes.

He did not set her down, but instead lifted her easily as he carried her with tireless strides.

"I saw things in the whirlwind," she said.

"What things?"

"Dark shapes. They swooped near us, but I could not make them out."

"The Thunderbirds and the Thunderhorses."

She knew of them. The Thunderbirds made the lightning by opening their eyes. The flapping of their wings and the great horses' beating hooves caused the thunder. "They're real?"

"Very. Watch as we travel and see what few humans

have witnessed. I call them in emergencies and they carry me. It is only by their good graces that I can fly."

"I couldn't get enough air. It's so cold."

"You did better. We traveled much farther before you fainted."

Not very reassuring, she thought.

Before them stood a small cabin constructed of plywood and two-by-fours. The square structure sat on raised on blocks cut from a large log. The exterior walls were painted kelly green, and the porch beams, formed from the nearby pines, were painted barn-red. Sebastian did not pause as he opened the door and stooped to cross the threshold.

He made a full circle in the room, before deciding to deposit her upon the bed. The room was cold and damp, so she drew her feet beneath her. He draped his heavy cloak around her shoulders. The weight of the garment practically pinned her to the spot. His scent and heat reassured her as she nestled deep into the fur.

He closed the door and went to work setting a fire. A full wood box, tinder and a lighter made the job easy for someone as experienced as Sebastian. Soon the little rectangular stove crackled to life and he swung the door shut, lowering the latch.

As the chill left the air, Michaela stood to explore her new surroundings. The floor was icy beneath the soles of her feet.

She glanced back at the bed she had vacated, noting it was no more than a large raised platform of plywood, covered with a piece of five-inch-thick foam. There was a sleeping bag, rolled at the foot, but no bedding and only one thin pillow. The wood-burning stove, set up on a rectangle of red bricks, lay centered on the wall across from the entrance. The firewood lay far enough away not to catch a stray spark. Above the stove, an empty clothesline crisscrossed the ceiling. Four mismatched wooden clothespins clung tenaciously to one strand. Two captain's chairs lay open before the stove, showing worn tan canvas of questionable strength.

The adjoining wall featured a long plywood counter holding a variety of jars and containers. Above this surface lay shelves filled with foodstuffs, pots and pans. Before the counter sat a small drop-leaf table with a green-and-white-checkered tablecloth of plastic that sported several cigarette burns. At the center a candle stub rested in a clean tuna can flanked by paper cylinders of salt and pepper sprinkled with a pattern of vegetables.

She retrieved the knapsack Sebastian had tossed near the table and hung her clothing on the line above the stove. Finally she set her boots on the brick hearth. Then she headed for the kitchen and went to work. After a few minutes she had unearthed vegetable shortening, pasta, a can of tomato sauce, biscuit mix, canned beans, coffee, tea, sugar and cans of peaches and fruit cocktail. A feast!

Sebastian ventured out to fill a cooler from a nearby spring and she collected plates and silverware, then opened the canned goods, which were frozen solid and required thawing on the stove. But the cast-iron stove took the chill from the room. She was warm for the first time since arrival.

He returned to find she had created a pasta dinner

complete with biscuits, vegetables and a peach cobbler, thanks to the brown sugar she discovered.

She didn't know which shocked her more, the speed with which Sebastian ate his dinner or the quantity of food he ate.

"Shall I make some more pasta?"

"Is there more?"

She cooked him a pound of elbow macaroni and he ate that with oil and a healthy pile of grated Parmesan cheese.

"How do you stay so thin?" she asked.

He raised a beefy arm and flexed. "I am not thin."

He wasn't. He was broad and strong and heavily muscled. No wonder he had the appetite of a sumo wrestler.

At last, Sebastian pushed away his dinner plate and sighed in contentment. "That was good."

She smiled at the Spartan praise.

"This from a man who says he will eat anything."

"That's true. But this tasted very good. Sweet and spicy things and things that are soft and chewy."

What an odd description. "You need to eat out more often."

"Mostly I eat what I find or kill."

She couldn't keep her eyes from widening at that.

"I only kill what I can eat," he assured her.

"You're a hunter, then."

He thought for a moment and then met her eyes with a glowing fire that made her stomach flutter and her blood course.

"Yes," he said.

She found her voice trembled at the intensity of his stare.

He leaned forward. "Recently, I have been hunting a soft little rabbit."

Her molten reaction to this made her spring to her feet. She had made this mistake already, and he had hurt her with his flight. She had had the brush-off before, but never with such blatancy. And now he acted as if he hadn't dropped her like yesterday's news the moment he recalled what they had done.

She met his gaze. It had been wonderful.

No, Michaela. Not again. You don't even know what he is. He's not human, that's certain, making him…what? An extraterrestrial? Yeah, right. An E.T. who knows Lakota folklore and travels with Thunderbirds.

She scooped up the dinner plates and took them to the stove, where she used the pot of warm water and a wet cloth to clean them. There was no food to discard, because Sebastian had eaten everything but the tin cans.

This was better. She didn't have to look at him. Instead, she focused on scouring the forks and spoons. His gaze was still on her. She could feel it as strongly as the heat from the woodstove.

Finally, there was no more delaying. She turned to face him, meeting the feral gaze and feeling her heart beat in her throat. He wanted her, hunted her, and there would be no escape.

The thought thrilled her, and she felt herself shiver with desire to have him once more.

"Shouldn't we go?" she asked.

He shook his head, his eyes never leaving hers. "It is too late to arrive. It would be rude."

"Oh." She pushed her hair away from her face.

"Come here," he ordered.

Chapter 15

Some part of her was still uncertain, still resisting this attraction that roared between them. If Michaela could keep him from knowing how much she truly wanted him, she might keep him from bedding her again.

That meant she could not let him touch her.

"You want me, Michaela. I know it."

She tried for a bluff. "I don't."

"Then why are your face and neck pink? Why are your lips already swollen, and why is your heart pounding there at your throat? Did you know I can smell your arousal?"

She backed away.

"Come here."

She took another step away, bumping the bed platform and folding onto the sheet of foam.

He rose and lifted the cloak from her shoulders. She did not know how he did it, but one moment he stood before her dressed in jeans and flannel, holding the cloak, and the next instant he stood gloriously naked before her except for his necklace. She gasped at the feast he presented her eyes.

His broad, muscular chest called for her to stroke it. Her gaze swept him, and her fingers itched to touch his golden skin. She glanced lower at his narrow hips and the thatch of hair surrounding his stellar erection. She felt herself flood with anticipation.

He was right to summon her. She couldn't keep herself from wanting what he offered, even knowing that he would hurt her again when this was finished.

He spread his arms in welcome, drawing her close, stroking her back. He reached for the hem of her dress. She raised her arms, but was not quite sure the dress was drawn away over her head. She only knew it was gone. She glanced to the ground but did not see it there. How had he done that?

"You're not wearing the pink lace."

She returned her attention to Sebastian. "No, that was wet."

"I'm glad I did not know it. I could not have concentrated."

"You know it now."

"Hmm," he said, stooping to clasp her bottom and draw her forward, controlling her, and moving her so he could kiss and lick his way down the sensitive flesh of her belly. His hands moved lower until his fingers found their way between her legs, stroking the sensitive flesh of her cleft.

She gasped and arched. He held her fast as she swayed, rocked by the inner storm.

His fingers delved within her as she leaned against his mouth. His tongue flicked out—the eye of her maelstrom.

"Oh, yes," she breathed, pressing hard against his questing mouth.

He kissed and fondled her until her knees buckled, but he held her there for his ministrations, helpless and wanting, as he brought her to the summit. There, the swirling flood of pleasure released. She cried out his name as her body went limp, yet still she wanted him inside her, wanted it more than anything she had ever wanted in her life.

He lifted her, cradled her and guided her open body over his. She was past ready to accept him. He stood and thrust into her, holding her with a strength that no longer surprised her. His steady hands clasped her hips, drawing her nearly to the limits of his length and then pulling her forward until their hips collided.

She looped her arms about his neck, but as his rhythm grew more insistent she relaxed her hold and let her body arch away, increasing the depth and pleasure of each stroke. She had never experienced lovemaking like this, never trusted a man to hold her this way.

His strokes grew faster and she relished each one. The realization that he traveled to the edge of his control but waited for her brought her to a second release. Her throaty moan undid him, for he pulled her tight, until their hips locked and held fast as he poured his seed into her wet passage. She relished the pulsing throb, feeling her own body rippling to bring him still deeper inside.

He moved his hands to her back and carried her to the bed. He laid her down and stretched out against her side, dragging the great fur cape over them like a blanket, encasing them in a warm nest. He turned her to her side and drew her back against him, bringing her bottom and back tight to his chest. One hand splayed against her breast, relaxed and warm.

They rested in the cabin, motionless as their breathing returned to normal.

Michaela wondered when they could do that again.

"Soon," he said, and closed his eyes.

She smiled and nestled close to him, feeling safe and loved. He had given her a great gift. He guarded her from those creatures who stalked her and she put her faith in him. If anyone could stop Nagi, it was Sebastian.

When she next came aware, the room was dark, but something moved beside her. Sebastian. She recognized his scent, his touch, the great broad comforting mass of him. She smiled as she realized what had awakened her.

He was ready for her once more. She felt the hard pressure of him against her thigh and shifted to press her belly to his groin.

"Can't a girl get some sleep around here?" She wrapped her fingers about his erection. His gasp gave her a smile of pure female satisfaction.

"What you do to me," he said, his voice husky.

"Oh, that's nothing." She licked her fingers, and then dragged them over the underside of his rigid flesh.

He groaned and pressed against her hand as his arousal twitched at the contact. Before she could stroke him again, he had her on her back.

She was going to protest, just to tease him, but her words died on her lips as she saw his eyes glittering in the dark. They glowed like a cat's at night. The words died on her lips as she took in the strange sight.

He positioned himself above her.

"No more word games, not when I feel your desire as strongly as my own."

She cast aside her uncertainty and inhaled at the rush of anticipation that came as she lifted herself to accept him. He dove forward with a force that pressed her deep into the foam mattress. He thrust with a speed that thrilled her, but raised the doubt that he could last long enough for her to find her pleasure.

"Never doubt it," he growled, and thrust. He released her hips to stroke her most sensitive flesh, driving her mad. She lifted herself, splaying her legs up over his shoulders to give him access to all of her.

She recognized the building desire, the urge to move, and at the same time to pause to relish the pleasure. It was coming now, no stopping it. The wave of fulfillment broke, crashing through her middle, rolling outward until it curled her toes. She cried his name in one long rushing release.

He drove into her slick passage, pushing forward as she lifted, bringing him to the base of her womb. He felt it. She could tell by the moment's hesitation. But there was no stopping as his body shuddered. He arched, sending his seed to her in a hot gush.

Her legs slid to his hips and he fell forward, collecting her as he rolled until she lay splayed across him like some living blanket. She had never felt more satisfied.

He held her in the quiet room as the last of her pleasure began to ebb.

His timing was spectacular.

"Thanks," he muttered, as if speech now was a great hardship.

She smiled. A possibility came to her along with a thrill at the thought.

"Can you feel my emotions, too?"

"Yes," he said.

"Did you feel my—"

"Yes."

Oh, my, he had experienced what she had. That realization made her hot all over again. He had shared her release and experienced his own.

"Triggering my own," he corrected.

She lifted a tired arm and stroked his head and back, reaching all the way to his wonderful, taut ass. Then she did it again.

"That was wonderful," she whispered.

He turned his face toward hers and she kissed his lips.

"I never knew females had such shattering experiences."

"Is yours so different?"

"It is—" he hesitated "—more focused. Like the difference between a thunderstorm and a lightning strike. Both have power in a different way."

She smiled and lowered her head to the cushion of his biceps. Contentment seeped around her like warm sand. He relaxed and dozed. Michaela nestled close to him, but her mind turned back to his glowing eyes. Her own popped open. The strangeness of him grew until her heart pounded with uncertainty.

Not a man.

Her fears rushed back, sweeping her along like a rudderless raft in a raging torrent. What terrible secrets did he hide? If she knew, she would leave him. That was what he told her, but nothing could be worse than the possibilities that were now threatening to overtake her. It was a different kind of madness, this dread. She was hunted by Nagi but had kept herself from his possession. Not so with Sebastian. He had possessed her, body and soul.

What had she done?

She felt physically sick. He could heal with a touch, and he could fly, call animals to do his bidding, and at night his eyes glowed like an animal's. She searched her mind for answers, recalling the Lakota myth. What if he was Iktomi, the prankster, or worse, Tuku Skanskan himself? The master of chaos could cause great sorrow to people. What kind of a monster had she given herself to?

She glanced at him and saw those unnatural eyes focused on her.

Sebastian glared down at her. "Monster?"

She lifted both hands to her throat as if choking. Her mouth dropped open, and he saw the same look of terror she had given him when he came to her as an animal. The same look his mother and wife had given long ago. Her glance darted from left to right, and she searched for a means to escape him. How could he blame her, when she had, at last, come to the right conclusion?

Her face flushed, and he could see it in the near dark, his eyes working far better than a human's.

"Sebastian?"

What was she thinking now, as she panted and quaked? Her expression was earnest and her eyes wide, offering hope. He reached, trying to reestablish their physical connection. At that level, he always understood her, but the fear made her eyes white and wide as she retreated to the wall, hands outstretched to ward him off.

He couldn't stomach it, to be the cause of such horror.

He grabbed for her, and she jumped away with surprising agility and lashed out. It was nothing to him, a tap, but he could see that the blow was her best effort to repulse him, as she was repulsed by him.

How could he blame her for feeling what he had long felt for himself?

He rose from the bed they had shared, backing away to give her the space she needed to face him. Seeing her tremble and knowing he was the cause tore at him like crows on a carcass.

"Sebastian, you must tell me what you are."

He shook his head, denying what he knew must come. She was frightened of the unknown. But that was preferable to seeing him turn. To show her was to lose her forever.

He stared at her. Had he not lost her already?

The tears came then, flowing in rivers down her cheeks. "Please, Sebastian. I know you are supernatural. And I know you are not a ghost. But the other possibilities…the doubt. It is worse than not knowing. I can't stand it any longer."

"Nothing is worse."

"You're wrong. This is cruel and you're not cruel by nature."

"I can be."

"I don't believe it."

Sebastian stood silently, veiling his gaze with his emotions.

She lifted her chin in defiance, showing her bravery or foolishness. He could not decide which.

"You have powers, strengths I don't understand, and you toy with me like a cat with a wounded bird."

"I said I could be cruel." Better for her to think that, believe it, than to know what it cost him to hurt her. It was like cutting his own flesh. He would do anything to protect her from pain, anything but show her the beast.

Her voice rose as she hurled words at him.

"Why didn't you leave me there?" She covered her tearstained face with her hands.

As if he could. But she would leave him, had left him already.

The truth of it crept through him on tiny feet, settling in the pit of his stomach.

She would abandon him regardless of what he did. Tell her, don't tell her, either way it was finished. All he had done was taste what he could never have.

This woman had made him feel human again. But she would run as soon as she could.

One look at her torment assured him that they could not continue as they had done.

He bowed his head in surrender.

It was why he did not travel with humans. It was too hard, too painful to see what could not be shared between them, the friendship, the trust, the understanding and, yes, the love. So he stood outside the fires of their camps, outside the limits of their cities, watching until it broke his heart, and then he retreated into the wild.

He backed toward the door, recognizing for the first time the heavy rain beating upon the roof. It seemed the sky cried with his little human. He had known he would hurt her, known he would disappoint her. Now it had come.

He turned to go, out into the storm, out into the wilderness that was his only refuge since his tribe had driven him away.

"Wait!"

She was tugging the flimsy pink top over her head, leaving her sex and her long, slim legs beautifully bare. Had it been only hours ago she had trusted him enough to wrap those long legs around him?

The yearning that swept through him nearly buckled his knees. But he bore it, as he bore all pain, in silence.

His first instinct had been right; she was far easier to pick up than to put down. But he had seen only her tiny body and not her powerful Spirit.

This weak and fragile little female had the strength to bring the great bear to his knees.

She reached for him, but now it was he who would pull back, no longer having the courage to read her thoughts.

"You're leaving me?"

"You don't understand."

She reached for the lantern on the table, striking a match and touching it to the wick. Yellow light flooded the cabin. "Please don't go. Stay and explain it to me. You tried to help me. I know it."

He scooped up his cloak, throwing it over his shoulders as he stepped out into the storm. Cold droplets pelted his naked flesh. There in the darkness, illuminated by the shaft of light stealing from the cabin, he faced her again.

No more deception. She would see what he truly was.

She followed now in her jeans with feet still bare, tenacious as a wolf pup clinging to a scrap. Michaela lifted the kerosene lantern high, revealing the worry etched on her brow and the confusion set in her searching gaze, but he also saw courage in the tilt of her chin and the shoulders drawn back to face this next challenge. It was what had attracted him initially, that audacious nerve in the face of Nagi. She would need it now, to face him.

He reached for his cloak and hesitated, recalling his mother's screams the first time she saw this. Was it the wind whistling in the branches, or did he hear her scream still?

Suddenly he was fourteen again, alone and confused as his mother fled from him as if he was Nagi himself.

"I'm sorry, Michaela."

"For what?"

"I'm sorry I could not be the man you deserve."

His hand came down upon his cloak, striking with a force that vibrated through his chest as he lashed out at himself with self-loathing.

At contact he felt the change. Swift as a diving peregrine, the energy of the Thunderbirds surged through his nerves, burning and snapping his head skyward. The rain pounded on his face as his claws tore from his nails and his coat grew to protect him from the storm.

He looked to the porch.

There she stood, frozen for one more moment. The lantern revealed her round, white eyes, her arm stiff as she held the light to expose him, still standing on two legs. He would never forget that look. It was the look she had cast on Nagi—the look of horror. Now she saw the truth and her expression killed any foolish hope he harbored that she might be different, might be strong enough to accept him for what he was.

How could he be so stupid?

She stood on the first step now, in the rain, holding the lantern high.

He wanted his animal mind to free him from this coursing agony. Why did it not come?

Always he had found escape from his human emotions in his animal half. But not now. Somehow she had broken the barrier between his two halves. Oh, sweet mystery, would he have to bear the agony of loss even as an animal?

He lifted his head and roared his raw pain to the heavens.

She staggered backward at his bellow, catching her leg on the porch. She caught herself, but the lantern fell, crashing down the steps, shattering on the ground. The kerosene blazed. The orange glow revealed her clutching both hands to her chest as if to protect her heart from him.

He wished he was like Bess and could speak from his

animal form, to tell her he would not harm her. He took an awkward, upright step in her direction and she collided with the cabin wall, clamping her hands to her ears and squeezing her eyes shut. He recognized this stance, had seen it before, just before his mother began screaming.

He dropped to all fours and fled before he could hear Michaela's screams.

Chapter 16

Michaela stared in stunned silence at the huge grizzly rearing up before her.

The bear dropped to all fours and ran.

The bear who had rescued her—he had not *called* the bear. He *was* the bear.

She leaped over the flames and ran out into the howling gale, chasing after him in the darkness. She could see him as the fire glinted off his wet fur. He reached the trees with unnatural speed and fluid grace.

"Sebastian! Wait!"

He vanished into the forest, and even as she ran, barefoot over the thick, spongy tundra tussocks, she knew she would never catch him. She dropped to her knees on the boggy cotton grass.

"Sebastian, don't go!"

Rain beat down, cold as slivers of ice upon her back, the camisole top sodden and clinging in the downpour.

The darkness closed around her. She glanced back the way she had come and saw the cabin porch blazing as the fire, protected by the roof, ate into the dry porch boards.

"No!" Michaela ran toward her only shelter.

She used the tarp from the woodpile to beat at the flames. But despite her efforts, the fire climbed up the upright pine beams, with the speed of rats boarding a ship, and began to eat at the rafters.

When she realized the cause was lost, her mind turned to salvage. Sebastian would come back. But how long would he be gone?

She tried not to entertain doubts. He would come, wouldn't he?

Until he did, she needed the supplies to survive. The flames already covered the front entrance. She ran around the cabin, to the side window, and used a chunk of firewood to break the glass. The sound could barely be heard above the thunderous downpour. She used a larger block of wood to climb up and through the window. The fire's light came through the front door and she wondered how long until the roof collapsed. Already smoke billowed along the ceiling. She threw objects out the kitchen window, beginning with the canned food and moving to pots, pans, water jugs, utensils, candles.

She dragged on her jeans, dry wool socks and slipped into her boots, snatching up the sleeping bag as the fire broke a hole through the roof. Was the rain inside dousing the fire that ate into the wooden structure like a hoard of termites?

Black smoke billowed all around her as she stuffed the lighter into the front pocket of her jeans.

Weapons. Did she have any?

The two kitchen knives flew out into the night, their silver blades catching the orange light of the blazing roof. How long before it collapsed?

The roar grew louder, but she could not tell if it was the crackle of flames or the beating of the rain upon the planks.

Her eyes burned from the smoke, forcing her to the window.

The crashing behind her convinced her that she had overstayed her welcome. The porch roof collapsed first, taking down part of the front wall.

She screamed as the cabin shifted. Michaela crouched with both hands over her head, but the side walls held.

The collapsing front wall trapped her between the flames and the solid cabin wall to her rear.

Michaela charged to the side window, praying the walls would hold her weight. She staggered onto the table, invisible now in the thick smoke. Her fingers registered the plastic tablecloth and she grasped it as she staggered toward the window, dragging the covering from its place and sending objects crashing to the floor.

She scrambled onto the counter. A breath of sweet, fresh air gave her hope that she might escape.

Michaela used the tablecloth to protect her from the

shards of glass littering the sill as she scrambled head-first out the narrow gap and into the torrent. Clutching the sill, she managed to hold on until her feet were below her and dropped to the ground. With a free hand, she snatched the green-checked plastic, whisking it away as she ran.

Flames shot into the air, rising high into the darkness. The front half of the cabin was engulfed.

Michaela dropped to her knees in the mud, lifting the tablecloth over her head and dragging the coiled sleeping bag under the meager cover. The rain beat on the plastic in a constant rhythm accentuated by her thick, wet cough. She was dizzy from the smoke that had burned her lungs and stung her watering eyes. She lifted a hand, noting it was coated with soot.

She had burned her only shelter to the ground. Michaela knew enough about the wild to know that without shelter she had little chance of survival.

She needed Sebastian.

She crawled to the trees, propping herself against the spindly trunk of the spruce and drawing the plastic down over her head as her mind turned to what she had witnessed.

Sebastian, her protector, was a Skinwalker. Such creatures could take the shape of a man, but the trick seldom worked because they were animals by nature and so could not fool men for long.

But he had fooled her. She had willingly dismissed all the inconsistencies.

Her lover, her savior, was a fearsome grizzly bear nearly twelve feet tall.

What had he said to her, that he was sorry he couldn't be the man she deserved?

Now it made sense: his strength and power, his attempts to be rid of her. He was not human, not really a man.

And yet she had slept with him—twice.

She sagged against the tree. What in the name of heaven and earth had she done?

Nagi was real, and Kanka, too. That meant the others were real as well. She pressed a hand over her mouth. Tob Tob. Had she lain with the great Spirit Bear himself?

What would happen now?

It made no sense. If such Spirits did exist, then they had taken measures to protect their identity from her race. To men, they existed only in lore. But they were real.

So why, of all the men and women of the world, was she the one they revealed themselves to?

Perhaps she wasn't the only one. There were the legends to prove that.

She wondered about it all, the Spirit Road and the other stories. Was this why her mother had tried so hard to teach her of her culture? Did she know that things were not at all what they seemed?

But if she knew they were real, then why hadn't she said so, told Michaela flat out?

Would you have believed her?

Another wall of the cabin crashed in and Michaela stared at the hungry orange flames as they battled the heavy rain for custody of the ruined structure.

The water would win, eventually. Already the fire hissed like a great snake, sending smoke billowing into the night sky, coiling and swirling.

Michaela held her breath.

It was the hiss of flame and water she heard. *Please let it be the fire.*

Her heart pounded as icy terror twisted within her. She was alone, vulnerable.

But that was when he always came. Yes, there was no mistaking him now, taking shape before her, gathering his substance from the fire. The smoke had a head and arms. The yellow eyes snapped open, pinning her with a ghostly, evil glare.

"Nagi," she breathed.

"I see you," he hissed, unable to contain his glee. He could smell her weakness now. His touch had eaten far into her Spirit, tearing the connection between flesh and soul. Soon her body would no longer be able to hold what would be his. Her end grew near.

Above him, his ghosts circled, called by her impending death. The odor was irresistible, drawing them to witness the separation of the soul from the vessel.

Each longed for that vessel, would try to take it as their own. But it was up to Nagi to decide who, if any, would have her discarded form.

Just a little longer and he would have her soul.

Sebastian ran nearly a mile before coming to a stop. He rose upon his hind feet and lifted his arms, changing back into the man he wished to be.

The heavy rain suited his dark mood. He had broken the rules of the Inanoka when he transformed before her. She had seen his true nature.

He had given her what she sought—the truth—and

he had lost her. His head drooped still farther. He would miss his little human.

His actions would force her to make a difficult choice. Stay with him a little longer or face Nagi alone? She would stay a little longer—wouldn't she?

He did not like this aching uncertainty gnawing inside him. How could he let her break his heart? He was strong. He did not need anyone. Hadn't his years of solitude proven he could live without a woman?

He turned and looked back the way he had come. He would have to face her again. He dreaded the encounter, but he started back. He could not cower like a cub. He was of the Bear Clan and bears faced all challenges head-on.

Her scream still rang in his ears.

He could almost hear it on the wind.

"Sebastian."

He stilled. The sound was faint, but he thought it was not his imagination…

"Sebastian! Help!"

He exploded into motion, charging over the tundra. The branches gave way, cracking and snapping as he barreled past at full speed. He ran down the steep hill, reaching full stride for the first time and topping thirty miles an hour, desperate to reach her. Now he smelled smoke, too much for a woodstove.

He recalled the lantern slipping from her hands and then the sound of breaking glass.

Sebastian stretched out his stride. She needed him. That was all he needed to know.

He broke into the clearing to find the smoldering

wreck of burning wood. There, using the black smoke to take shape, Nagi billowed, menacing Michaela, who lay motionless upon the ground.

Sebastian roared his fury and charged. Nagi turned his evil yellow eyes on him as Sebastian attacked, but his blows went through the wraithlike body of Nagi.

"Go away, Inanoka," he growled. "You have lost."

Sebastian swung again. Nagi's body reassembled behind the blow.

"Do you think to keep this frail one? Ha!" Nagi undulated before him. "Find another, little cub, for this one is already mine."

Sebastian lunged, breaking through the wall of acrid smoke that was Nagi. The ruler of the ghosts reconverged as soon as he had passed.

"All you did was slow the inevitable. Each time I come, she is closer to death. You cannot stop it, for my power is greater than yours."

Everything Nagi said was true, but none of that would keep him from trying to save her. He would stand between Michaela and this terrible end. It was not enough, but he would do all he could because for the first time in his life he knew where he belonged—here by her side.

"You can't have her."

Nagi laughed. "Can't I?"

He lifted a ghostly hand. Behind him, Michaela screamed. Above him, the whirling dark smoke reeked of death. Ghosts, he realized.

The smoke gave him an idea. She was not strong enough for such a journey, but to stay was to watch her die.

He did not deliberate. He knew this might kill her, but his instinct told him to act and so he did. He scooped up her limp form from the sodden earth and closed his powerful arms around her, then he raised his head and bellowed to the heavens, calling to the Thunderbirds.

They came.

The huge flapping wings sent Nagi swirling like smoke from a pipe. The screech of the great birds' call caused even Nagi to tremble. They swooped from the west and lifted Sebastian and Michaela into the sky.

Nagi tried to follow, but they beat him back with their mighty wings, sending him into a swirling vortex that was too great even for him.

Michaela stirred in Sebastian's arms and her eyes fell open. She looked up at him with eyes wide and bulging, like a creature held under the water. He knew she could not breathe, that he was killing her, and he urged his friends to greater speed.

Michaela looked around her. Did she see the great birds? If a human even glimpsed them she would be Heyoka, with healing powers and the ability to understand the messages in dreams.

She struggled now, fighting for her life as he held her safe from the whirlwind.

Hurry, he thought. *Hurry or she will die.*

About him the wind raged, stronger than he had ever felt, so fierce that he fought for each breath in the icy air. He drew it in, warming it in his great lungs, and then opened his jaws, covering her nose and mouth with his, and exhaled. Did she receive the breath warmed by his body?

He tried again, growing dizzy with the effort. His last thought was to lock his great arms around Michaela, protecting her even in death.

Chapter 17

The winds had ceased. Michaela drew a ragged breath and then another. The tingling gradually disappeared from her fingers and toes as oxygen flowed through her bloodstream.

The air was icy, but she pressed against something warm. She tried to lift her head, but her body would not respond to her mind's command. She felt woozy and weak, as if she had been drugged. It took great effort to open her eyes. Finally, she managed this small act of consciousness.

Hair brushed her cheek. She blinked, taking in the ice frosting the dark brown fur that blew in the bitter wind. She stared at the massive body and then turned her head, noticing the grizzly's forearms wrapped around her. He sheltered her from the cold by holding her up against his body. She craned her neck.

The sun hung low and pale on the flat horizon. What she noticed next was not what was, but what was not. There were no trees or hills or mountains to obstruct the view, only blue ice as far as she could see.

It had been night when they left, hadn't it? How long had she been lying on the ice? How long had they been traveling?

What was this place?

"Sebastian?"

No response. She tried a tentative shove but got no reaction. What if he were dead? She pressed her ear to his chest. The reassuring rhythm of his steady heartbeat removed the lump of panic from her throat and she sagged with relief.

He had come back to her, saved her from Nagi once more.

But now he needed her help. She wiggled and pushed, managing to drag herself from beneath the weight of his huge forearm. Immediately she was sorry. Her wet clothes were no protection in this hostile environment.

Why had he brought her here?

"Sebastian." She rocked his shoulder, but he did not rouse.

Would he know her, as a bear? She burrowed next to him, weeping. He must know her, he must.

He lay immobile on the icy ground, exhaling in great, steady puffs of frost. Here he was—her Skinwalker.

She stroked his face. "Oh, Sebastian."

He was not a man at all. Yet she trusted him. No, this

was more than trust. Knowing the truth of what he was did not change that.

She rested her cheek upon his thick neck, drawing warmth and comfort from him.

"Why won't you wake up?"

"Because he used all his strength to carry you through that storm." The voice was harsh as cracking ice, but with a melodic cadence that reminded her of a chanted prayer.

Michaela turned to see the round face of a woman wrapped from forehead to heel in white furs. She looked Inuit with a moon face that glowed with an unnatural translucency as if carved of ivory. The parka hood fringed her face with the grayish-white fur of a timber wolf. The long soft hairs radiated out from her head like the rays of a sun. She was stooped, making her look like a hunchback, and she wore shapeless fur pants and high sealskin boots, with fluffy white pom-poms at the laces. She braced both hands on an elaborately carved white ivory cane that resembled a totem pole, with one Arctic animal stacked upon the next.

"I am Kanka. Sebastian brought you to me. Come in, child."

In? Michaela glanced past her, seeing for the first time the large pile of bones. She recognized the jaws of whales all around the perimeter. How did they get here?

Michaela crawled to her feet, then stopped. "What about Sebastian?"

Kanka laughed. "Can you carry him?"

Michaela shook her head.

"Best leave him, then."

Michaela hesitated.

"He's a bear, honey. Cold won't do him no harm." She motioned with a hand sheathed in a heavy gauntlet-style glove. "He'll be along by and by."

Michaela cast her worried gaze on him. "Are you certain?"

"Land sakes, child, is he protecting you or are you protecting him? Come now, or you'll freeze solid. It's forty below out here." Without waiting, Kanka turned to go.

Michaela noted the frost stiffening her jeans and the ice crystals coating her hair like dripping wax.

Kanka paused. "Cold up here all the time. Best follow me now."

Michaela did, glancing back twice to see that Sebastian had not moved.

Kanka walked spryly to her abode, stabbing the point of her stick in the ice as she went. She reached a huge walrus skin hung across the entrance and tossed it back as she entered, as if it weighed no more than a down sleeping bag.

"Flip that back once you're in," she called, and disappeared into the dark.

Michaela followed, then struggled to lower the hide back into place only to find herself in total blackness for an instant, until Kanka lifted another skin at the opposite end of a short tunnel, allowing a glimpse of a light.

"Let's get you out of those things."

Kanka set out a tan dress and chocolate-colored fur mukluks, each adorned with a beaded star. Michaela hesitated only for as long as it took to begin to shiver and then stripped out of her stiff attire and slipped into the soft sleeveless hide dress.

"I've never worn buckskin before."

Kanka smiled, draping Michaela's shoulders with a quilt made of different fur pelts. "And I'm sure you'd look lovely in it, but this is sealskin. We don't have many bucks this far north, 'less you count caribou, and they don't come this far up, generally. Long trip to find them and I prefer to stay here. Seal, walrus, whale and sometimes a bear." She glanced toward the entrance. "They suit me. No reason to go tromping over the ice."

Michaela wondered how a lone woman caught a whale and then recalled all the bones Kanka used to construct her home. Something inside Michaela tensed—misgivings mixed with a healthy dose of alarm.

Michaela slid into the soft fur-lined boots and had to stifle a groan of pleasure. They felt so extravagant and warm to her icy feet.

The distraction of being out of her frozen clothing kept Michaela from immediately noting that Kanka's fire was not orange as it should be, but glowed a pale blue-green, like seawater aflame. The bleached wood she thought she saw upon entering, she now recognized was not wood at all, but the long bones of some animal.

Michaela cast her hostess a worried look.

"What kind of fire is that?"

Kanka laughed, showing long white teeth, filed to menacing points. Michaela drew back, feeling queasy. These were the teeth of a predator, not human—no, not nearly human.

Michaela's disquiet grew as the sorceress removed

her parka, revealing waist-length hair that was not white or gray, but silver as polished sterling. Her eyes were wrong as well, gray with the dull metallic shine of pewter. This discovery made Michaela glance toward the door for Sebastian.

"He'll be along. He's waking now. In the meantime, let me see that wound."

"How did you know?"

"Oh, I can sense it, child. That tear in your flesh is pulling your soul from your body. You feel it. That's what makes you all woozy and remote."

She had felt it. The icy dread broke in a cold sweat across her brow. This injury threatened her existence; she knew it but did not know how.

Kanka drew back the quilt she had offered and then removed the bandage. Green glowing pus once more oozed from the gap in the black wound, but now the skin from her shoulder to her wrist looked gray, like the flesh of a corpse.

A flutter of panic stirred in her belly and she bit her lip to keep it from trembling.

"Nagi's mark."

"Can you help me?"

"Always can help, but I can't bring everything back like it was, like you're hoping. Things change all the time. They're changing fast in you." Kanka turned away and began rummaging in leather pouches, drawing out bits of bone, metal containers and folded leather parcels. "You wondering why this is all happening, that right?"

The strange pewter eyes stared at her, alive, yet not

alive. Michaela tried to cease her trembling, failing even to keep her voice steady when she spoke.

"I had an accident."

"You died, child, twice. Started along the Spirit Road. Not too far, but far enough for Nagi to get a real good look." Kanka took a bit of what looked like charcoal and crushed it into her palm with the thumb of her opposite hand. "This here is charred raven bone. Helps you remember things." She lifted her open hand and blew the black dust into Michaela's face just as Michaela inhaled.

She choked as the powder burned her throat and made her eyes water.

"Think back, child. Now you can remember."

Michaela clasped her head as lightning flashes exploded behind her eyes. What was happening?

"You see that trail in your mind's eye?"

She did, a path of stars stretched out before her in a familiar track, and she felt as if she were going home. Her father, she sensed him, and her mother. But that was wrong; her mother had still been alive then.

Kanka's voice intruded. "Stop all that thinking. Just remember."

Then the shadow fell across the trail. Nagi coming for her, trying to take her where she did not belong. She had turned and run down the trail, back to her body and back to the pain.

"That's right. Now you see. Your daddy, he protected you, shielded you when you were just a baby, so Nagi, he never knowed about you. Think back now, to the last time you seen your daddy."

Michaela felt dizzy with the rush of visions. She was young, not yet three, when her father had abandoned them.

"You're thinking again. Look around, child."

She closed her eyes and felt herself perched on her mother's hip looking at her father as he chanted. Her mother's grip tightened and her voice came from behind Michaela.

"Is it done?"

Her father nodded. "I've seen to it. She won't feel her powers for two decades."

"But what about you?"

She heard the anguish in her mother's voice, but did not understand.

"He's seen me and he'll come. I can't hide. All I can do is lead him away and hope I'm strong enough to survive."

Mother was crying now and so Michaela cried with her.

Her father stroked her cheek. "Keep her safe, and if anything happens to me, do what you promised."

He pressed in to hug them, and Michaela recognized the familiar scent of him, recognizing it instantly after all this time.

Michaela stared at Kanka in shock.

"He didn't abandon us. He left to protect me."

Kanka leaned forward, so the flames cast her in a strange green glow. "You have the gifts of your father—the power to see ghosts."

Michaela shook her head in denial. "Only since the accident."

"No, child, always. Your daddy, he just veiled your powers, so you wouldn't think to use them. He knew this force runs both ways. You see them. They see you."

"You mean I'm some kind of psychic?"

"No, you can't read minds or see the future. You're a Seer of the Soul—any kind of soul once it leaves the body."

"The good ones all go to the Spirit World. I only see the evil ones."

"That's not so. You'll see all kinds. There are four. First is the ones still connected by love. They been torn from someone, someone they just can't be parted from. So they wait. No harm in that. This kind of ghost watches over those they love, keeping them safe until their time comes, so they can walk the Spirit Road together. The second kind is confused. They don't know they has passed because they was torn from their body unexpected like. So they goes around looking for that life and pretending they is still a part of things. Then there's the wronged ones, ones that has been murdered. Some move on, but others stay to haunt them that stole that life. These ghosts wait to see their killers pushed from the Spirit Road after they pass. That's their right. Last one is the kind you been seeing—the bad ones. They done wrong. Bad wrong and they knows they is already destined to walk the Circle."

"But why are they here?"

"They's hiding. Least, they used to be hiding, and Nagi, he come by periodically and collect them. But Nagi, he ain't doing his job. He's not collecting them no more. What we's got to figure is why. These souls, they be desperate to stay on earth, to taste the life they lost. Now, if Nagi, hisself, has given his blessing, standing by while they take possession of animals and folks, who's gonna stop them?"

She didn't even hesitate. "Sebastian."

Kanka shook her head. "He can smell them some, but can't force them out without nearly killing the possessed. No, child, he can't stop this." Kanka stared at her. "Don't you see it child? It's you."

"Me?"

"You can see them *before* they take a body and you can send them to the Circle. You must be awful powerful, 'cause Nagi wants you real bad."

Michaela spoke with a voice ringing with incredulity. "Me?"

"Yes, you."

"But I don't know how to do that."

"Yet." She smiled. "Your father knew and you got all his gifts. No choice about that. He must have known Nagi would be wanting you, 'cause he hid you as best he could, blocking your powers and telling your mama to hide you if he went missing, which he did. Hard for her to leave you, but she done it like she promised. Saved your life, she did. 'Cause when Nagi found her she never told about you. So Nagi, he never known you existed till you come traipsing along the Spirit Road, right by his Circle. Now he's coming after you."

"But my mother didn't leave me. She only died a few months ago."

"That weren't your birth mother, but your aunt. When her man went missing, she left you with her sister, like she promised, told her, 'Teach this one the old ways.'"

Michaela sat back on her heels as everything she believed was ripped out from under her in some bad imitation of a magician's trick with the tablecloth. Her whole world tilted dangerously.

"But..."

"Think back. They're in there."

Michaela recalled a face, her mother's, similar to her aunt's, but her eyes were green and her hair blunt-cut. She saw them both now, her mother and father, and knew it was true—all of it.

"Ah, you see them?"

"But this makes no sense. I don't have any powers and I'm certainly no threat to Nagi."

"You like a baby killer whale. Don't know how fast she can swim or how hard she can bite. You don't know 'cause you never been schooled. Your kind is trained from birth to use their gifts. But not you. It's the sacrifice your father made to keep you safe. Good choice, 'cause you still breathing. He veiled your gifts until you turned twenty-three."

"But I'm only twenty-one."

Kanka touched the place where Michaela had split open her skull. "He never figured on you walking the Ghost Trail and then coming back."

"My accident...it opened the connection."

"Now they see you and Nagi, he sees you as a threat."

"A threat to what?"

"I don't know. But he's up to something, leaving his Circle and keeping those monsters in this world. Ask me, they had no right to walk the earth the first time, let alone get another go-round."

"Kanka, what am I?"

"You're the child of human mother and father, who

was descended from the Spirit God, Niyan. You are a Spirit Child, half-human, half-Niyan. They calls themselves Niyanoka, and all have gifts, not all the same gifts, you understand."

She absorbed the enormity of this, feeling as if the world had suddenly fallen squarely on her shoulders.

"Does Sebastian know what I am?"

She shook her head. "He thinks you're human—his human. Marked you good and proper, didn't he?"

Michaela blushed.

"He did right bringing you to me. But he won't keep you if Nagi has his way."

Michaela flinched as if Kanka had punched her in the solar plexus.

The woman's nearly invisible eyebrows rose. "But you don't go down quiet. Hear? You're powerful, else Nagi wouldn't pay you no mind."

"But I'm not trained. You said I should have learned since childhood."

"Didn't say it would be a fair fight." She lifted her strange mercury eyes to Michaela. "Nagi wants to send you to the Spirit World." She stirred her fire absently, staring down at the glowing coals. "You the only one with the power to stop him."

Michaela pointed to the green embers. "Can you see him there?"

"No child. It's not my gift. I see pieces of life working as a whole, past, present, future. I see Nagi threatens the balance. That's why I'm gonna help you all I can."

Cold air blew all around her, and she turned to see Sebastian drawing back the hide curtain and stepping into the room. His height prevented him from standing upright, and still his presence filled the space.

He wore his heavy fur coat that she now knew was made of his own skin, high sealskin boots, black form-fitting trousers, a thick brown sweater and gloves.

"Sebastian." She breathed the word like an answered prayer.

His gaze scanned her from head to toe, and then he exhaled his breath. His eyes pinned her, regarding her with a cautious expression, as if trying to judge her mood. He came no closer.

She did not make him wait. Yes, she had seen him transform, but more important, he had snatched her from Nagi. She felt his benevolence and understood that he would not hurt her. Now she realized why he lived alone, kept to himself and struggled so hard with the decision to help her. He was different from humans, just as she was.

She ran to him, and he opened his arms wide, accepting her as she threw herself into his embrace. He clasped her to his side and rocked gently back and forth. To Michaela, it felt like coming home.

His head dropped to the top of hers and he drew her close, rubbing her back with long comforting strokes. This was what she longed for all her life, without even knowing, this kind of acceptance and trust.

"I was afraid I had killed you," he whispered.

"You saved me."

He drew back to stare into her eyes. "You do not fear me, little rabbit, now that you have seen what I am?"

Chapter 18

Sebastian waited in agony. How had he let this little human become the center of his world? She had tunneled into his heart with the determination of a prairie dog expanding her burrow.

She smiled up at him. "I trust you with my life."

He gasped in astonishment. The terror and the loathing he had dreaded had not come. She accepted him. It was a gift he could never have expected. Even Nicholas, with his many human conquests, had never tasted such joy.

She was smiling at him—at him, a Skinwalker, only half-human.

Kanka coughed and he glanced to her for the first time, only just recalling she was there. She did not smile; in fact, the look she cast them smacked distinctly of disapproval. He didn't care. He was glad that Michaela knew what he was. If Kanka could heal her and if Michaela would accept him, he would stay with this woman all her life.

He stepped back to scrutinize her and noticed the grayish skin surrounding Michaela's wound. Prickling anxiety crawled over his body like an army of ants. He looked to Kanka, his question upon his face.

"Can you heal this wound?" asked Sebastian.

"I can heal the place where evil touched her soul, though she will bear a mark."

Sebastian was not certain by her answer that she could cure Michaela, but he was desperate for her help.

"Do it, then," he ordered.

Kanka's smile was menacing. "You show yourself as more animal than man. I will do what I will do, with or without your bidding."

He had inadvertently insulted her. He chose the submissive path and glanced away, breaking contact with her unnatural eyes.

Kanka continued to berate him. "What are you, Sebastian, over one hundred? But still you haven't learned manners, because you do not walk often as a man. Do you?"

He felt Michaela's grip tighten at the disclosure of his age.

"One hundred?" she asked.

"One-ten," he admitted.

Her wide eyes were back. She stood right beside him, but he felt her slipping away. He could not bear the confusion in her mind. He turned to Kanka.

"I am sorry."

"Yes, you are, and over your head, just like a bear. Not used to being bested. But you never faced a foe like this one. Nagi's stronger than me and I've beaten a bear or two in my time." She pointed to the large skull by the fire.

Sebastian instantly recognized the remains of a polar bear, a big one. He cautioned himself. Kanka had great power and a hair-trigger temper. She was unpredictable and she was Michaela's only hope.

"Will you heal this woman?"

Kanka's grin and the maniacal twinkle in her eyes did nothing to assure him. Rather, it made him brace, preparing to take Michaela and run if the sorceress turned ugly.

"I can heal her Spirit, but the wound has torn the fabric that joins her body and soul. Only she can bring them together."

"No human can do such a thing."

"True." The smile broadened. "But she is not human, bear."

Now it was *his* face masked in confusion. She was not Inanoka for he recognized his own by scent. He glanced from Michaela to Kanka.

Kanka laughed at his befuddlement. "She is Niyanoka."

Sebastian staggered back as if from a body blow.

A Spirit Child—the other Halfling breed. Niyanoka did not associate with his kind—not ever. They did not trust and they did not love. It had been so since the war between their races.

He swallowed back the lump in his throat.

Michaela came toward him, hands reaching.

"Sebastian, what is it? What has happened?"

"The little cub understands. He must give you up."

Michaela sputtered in confusion. "But, but...he saved me. He kept me alive. Why would he do that if—"

"'Cause he loves you," said Kanka. "Without even knowing what you are. But now he sees that he can never have you and it burns him like fire." She stared at him as if studying an ant under a magnifying glass. "It's true, then. Inanoka do have hearts, for I see yours bleed." Her smile was cold. "Go into the snow and hunt, bear. I do not work for free. Bring back something big. I hunger for red meat."

He staggered toward the entrance to do her bidding, unsteady as if shot by a high-powered rifle.

"Sebastian?" Michaela's voice trembled. "What is happening?"

He shook his head. He still wanted her, even knowing he could never have her. He had marked her as his mate, hoping she might accept him. And by some miracle she had, even after seeing him transform. But she was Niyanoka.

How could fate be so cruel? Kanka would heal her, and he would have no choice but to do what he had planned to do all along—return her to the place where he had found her and let her go.

He turned away, but she grasped him, clinging with all her tiny human strength. He could shake her off, disappear out the door and never look back. But instead, he found the unnatural urge to scoop her up and run into the twilight.

Her face shone earnestly up at him. He had found a

human female to love him, but she was no more human than he was.

"I don't understand," said Michaela. "Where are you going?"

Her bewildered gaze broke his heart, but when her bare hand touched his cheek, he read the volcano of confusion erupting inside her. It was too much. He drew away.

Kanka's admonishment came from behind them. "Leave her, bearling. She was not raised by her kind and does not understand their ways."

He tried to step back and still she clung, tenacious as a weasel scenting blood.

He did not know where he found the courage to speak. His voice came as more growl than words as his animal side chafed against such rules and conventions.

Michaela tugged at his arm. "This doesn't change anything between us."

That she still thought to stay with him after learning the truth only showed that she had no understanding. It would have been easier to see her disgust than to bear witness to her stubborn insistence that all could be as it was. She met his gaze and saw the realization that he was going. She clasped her hands to his cheeks, searing him with her pain at his abandonment.

"No," she begged.

"Let go now," he whispered.

She did, thank Maka. He stroked her cheek with the index finger of his hand. "Stay with Kanka until I return."

Her hand slipped off the fur of his coat and she stood looking lost and alone. The sight broke his heart.

He gritted his teeth and headed out into the snow.

* * *

Michaela turned to the old sorceress. "What did you say to him? Where has he gone?"

"He seeks payment for my services for he knows you cannot."

Michaela recalled the look of absolute loss on his face. It hung over her like a shadow on her heart. Why did he look so crestfallen? What were they talking about? "He will be back, then?"

She nodded, her sharp eyes pinned on Michaela as if she were prey. "But it is as you fear. All has changed between you."

"Why did he look at me like that?"

"Like you tore out his intestines with your bare hands? You are descended of Niyan. That means you are a Halfling, like him, but not like him. His people protect the animals. Yours help humans. There are clans among your people, too, but unlike the Inanoka, your clans are not named after animals. You alone are Ghost Clan."

"Ghost?"

"The very last one. Clans come from the mother's side, so you might not always be the last. Still long odds against you unless you learn how to use them gifts. But if you die, none on earth will see them ghosts sneaking about."

Michaela felt a chill and moved closer to the unnatural fire. She did not want such a horrible gift. She wanted to fly like the Thunderbirds or heal like Sebastian.

"But Sebastian can see ghosts. I know he can."

"No, child, he can see Spirits, like Nagi. All Halflings can. But Spirits aren't ghosts. Spirits are the first creation of Wakan Tanka, the Great Mystery, so they is immortal and mighty. Ghosts is just what's left over once the body drops away. Sebastian can't see them 'cause it ain't his job. He's got to protect all those that go on four legs, while you watch over those that goes on two."

Michaela frowned in confusion.

"Though you go on only two, so it is not his concern, but the bear was in danger so he stops. All Halflings gotta try to keep humans from learning of their existence. Once he seen your Spirit Wound threaten that secret, he should have left you or killed you. As I said, it don't figure." Kanka lifted a knobby bone that looked like a vertebra of something large, for she hefted it in two gnarled hands as she held it over a metal bowl. Then she crushed the bone to dust as if it were chalk.

Michaela shrank back in surprise, reminded in that instant that Kanka was not an old woman living in an odd house. She was a supernatural creature with powers beyond understanding.

Michaela trembled.

"We'll make you that medicine now," she said, and winked. As she leaned forward, a strange pendant slipped from beneath her parka.

For a moment Michaela thought it was clear glass, but then she noticed it was moving, swirling like a hurricane as seen from a Doppler radar image.

"What is it?"

"Just a no-name storm. Nobody missed it." She tucked it back under her robe.

Michaela felt her skin prickling a warning, only the feeling was stronger, bordering on painful.

"That's one of your gifts, too. You can see Supernaturals and all Spirits, not just Nagi. That prickling is your alert. You feel that and you look around. Shouldn't be too hard to spot us." Kanka lifted the bowl. "Now, let's heal that ugly mess on your arm. My magic will close up the flesh, but it will also open up the portal to your gift. When I'm done, you'll be able to see all ghosts. See 'em, talks with 'em, even send them packing, once you learns how. Though if it were me, I'd only send off the ones that are confused or the ones that done wrong. The others—I think they got a right to linger."

Kanka lifted the bowl and Michaela shrank back, suddenly fearful. She wished Sebastian was here to protect her, for she did not trust this sorceress.

Kanka laughed, and Michaela's eyes narrowed in suspicion. Could the woman read her thoughts?

"You got little choice. We heal that and you get your gift or we don't heal it and you die. Now, give me that arm."

Michaela was so dumbfounded she merely extended her arm. It was too much to take in. She was Niyanoka of the Ghost Clan and a Seer of Souls. What did Seers do? She opened her mouth to ask and spotted the bowl of powdered bone before her.

A flash of foreboding shook away her questions. Kanka neither mixed the bone dust into some potion nor burned it in her fire, as Michaela expected.

Instead, she lifted another bone and struck it sharply against the rim of the metal bowl. A low gong vibrated through the air. Kanka spun the bone along the inner rim, bringing forth a deep rolling hum from the metal. The powdered bone in the basin rose up, swirling in a sparkling white minitornado like snowflakes twinkling in the sunlight. The beauty of the motion captivated Michaela. She gasped, and then leaned forward to get a better look at the dancing dust. She saw an animal there, a sperm whale, diving and breeching in the swirling particles.

Then it dove deep, disappearing into the vessel. Michaela leaned farther forward to catch a glimpse of the phantom whale. It rose with a speed that forced her to lurch back. The specter left the spinning tornado above the bowl and dove toward her. She lifted her arms up to defend herself, and the whale opened its leverlike mouth, showing rows of gleaming silver teeth as it latched on to her wounded arm.

Michaela screamed and tried to shake it off, but it clamped down harder, thrashing until it dug so deeply into her flesh that only the tail waggled obscenely from her open wound.

"Get it off me!" she screamed.

But Kanka only watched with malevolent eyes.

Michaela felt something else now, branching out in all directions from her wound, gripping at her flesh as if many arms wrapped around her muscles and corded around her blood vessels. The whale's tail thrashed violently as it slowly retreated, emerging from her arm. It gripped something black in its mouth. The thing flailed, clinging to her flesh like tar until she thought it would tear the very vessels from her arm.

The whale bit harder, and the black thing released its hold on her, withdrawing in long strands that reminded her of tentacles. The whale sailed back through the air, aiming for the bowl, still clutching its prize. It joined the swirling vortex, swimming in rising circles.

Michaela stared at the obscenity gripped in its crushing jaws. The struggling black mass had taken the shape of a giant squid, with familiar yellow eyes. Its long tentacles latched around the whale in a death struggle. The whale reached the pinnacle of the spinning crystals and dove straight into the vortex of the whirlpool until it hit the bottom of the bowl, making it ring like a bell.

At the sound, the white powder fell innocently back into the container. Quick as a thief, Kanka snatched up the vessel and hurled the contents into the fire.

There was a flare of violet flames and then a hiss of yellow sparks before the erupting of black smoke.

"Nasty one."

"Was that a squid in my arm?" asked Michaela, still blinking in astonishment at the fire.

"It was Nagi's magic. Strong and black. But my whale, he's strong, too. Took me three days to land him."

"You landed a sperm whale by yourself?"

Kanka grinned, showing both her pride and menacing rows of pointed teeth.

Michaela felt sick to her stomach, and she was overtaken with a deep longing to lie in her bed and draw her blankets over her head. Instead, she faced her terrifying hostess.

"Thank you."

The sorceress glanced at the open wound. "We best close that. It will heal now."

She reached in a leather pouch and withdrew a bone needle and black thread. Michaela drew back.

"The skin is still numb. You won't feel it," said Kanka.

Michaela looked away as the sorceress went to work closing the flaps of skin. As promised, Michaela felt no pain, but the tugging disquieted her. At last Kanka pulled the cord taut and sliced it with a bite from her wicked teeth.

"Stitches stay in. No need to pick at them."

"They dissolve?"

"No." Kanka grinned. "They join with your skin."

Michaela glanced at her arm and saw the stitches form two bisecting lines, one horizontal and one vertical. Surrounding them, the punctures of the bear's teeth formed a rough circle.

"It looks like a wheel," said Michaela.

"A medicine wheel," corrected Kanka. "Appropriate for a Seer of Souls."

She drew out a tin of a white cream, which she smeared liberally over the wound.

"More bone?"

The old sorceress laughed. "This is zinc oxide, child. It's real good on burns and cuts."

Michaela laughed, as well, only hers sounded hysterical and frightening to her ears.

"I'll see ghosts now?"

"No, child, that will take one more spell. But you best rest while you can. Nagi will know I broke his magic and be mad as a tundra chicken in a rainstorm."

Michaela glanced around the circular hut, searching for a moving shadow with glowing yellow eyes.

Kanka laughed. "He won't dare come here."

"Are you more powerful than he is?" She couldn't keep the hope from her voice.

"Not more powerful, exactly. See, I'm more like a skunk. Not the strongest or fastest, but creatures keep their distance round me or regrets it. Only the foolish ones tangle with me, and Nagi, he's not foolish. No, he sure is not."

"Can you help me defeat him?"

"Defeat him? Mercy, child, you can't. Best you can do is bring him to a draw, like that silly bear. Nagi tried to possess him and learned something new. But you could have done worse. Without that grizzly, Nagi would have you already."

"Can you teach me how to 'bring him to a draw,' then?"

"My way ain't your way. You're no skunk. But all creatures have means to survive. You have to learn your way and hope you're prepared when he come. If I were him, I'd come sooner, hoping to catch you before you ready."

"How will I learn, then?"

"That should've been your daddy's job. But he had to go poking around where he don't belong. Cost him dear. So they're gone from you until you walk the Spirit Road yourself." Kanka lifted Michaela's chin with a bony finger.

Michaela had to repress a shudder at the wintry touch; the woman was as cold as the ice on which she lived.

"Don't look so glum, child. There's a teacher for you. Teach you the laws of your kind and ways to keep humans from seeing what you truly are. When I'm done, you go to your people."

"What about Sebastian?"

"What about him?"

"I can't go without him."

"You best set him from your mind, child. You're a fine Niyanoka, and he's just a bear that knows how to walk on his hind legs. You're not for the likes of him."

"Don't you say that!" Michaela could not contain her rage.

For some reason, Kanka seemed pleased at her outburst, for her mouth quirked. Then she cast a quick look at her fire and stirred the coals, staring into the green embers as if reading a map. After a moment her sharp eyes shifted back to Michaela.

"Well, well, now. 'Never been' don't mean 'never will be,' do it, girl?" Kanka rubbed her nubby chin as she studied Michaela. Her muttered words seemed more for her own benefit than for her guest's. "Things is about to get real interesting round here."

Chapter 19

Kanka lifted something from the coals and offered Michaela what looked distinctly like an upturned tusk of a walrus.

She hesitated, then accepted the offering, glancing with suspicion at the milky-white fluid within. It was rude to ask what it was, but after the diving whale she wondered if she dared.

Kanka grinned. "Best to be cautious, but there's no magic in that cup, just nourishment. Make you strong so you can heal that gash."

Michaela could read nothing in her quicksilver eyes as she placed the odd cup to her lips and drank. The warm fluid tasted sweet.

"Reindeer milk," said Kanka.

Well, that didn't sound too bad.

"And blood," she added as an afterthought, making Michaela choke.

Michaela lowered the nearly empty tusk, feeling queasy. Kanka's lips twitched in a hint of a smile. Michaela got the distinct impression that she knew exactly what effect her words would have. Next she offered a large wooden bowl filled with a steaming liquid.

"*Ooyuk,*" she said. "Seal soup with kelp."

"And blood?" asked Michaela, staring warily at the clear broth.

"Not this time. Just kelp and fermented seal."

Michaela was concerned over the fermented part, but her stomach chose this moment to grumble loudly. She tipped the bowl and drank the salty broth, then picked out the generous chunks of meat and ate them one by one. They were chewy and salty, with a tang that she feared was not spice. The meal complete, she waited anxiously for her stomach to rebel, but it seemed content with the unusual meal.

Michaela wondered why Kanka did not eat. All sorts of odd explanations popped into her head. Perhaps she didn't eat. She was immortal, after all.

"Are you hungry, Kanka?"

"Very."

All the tales of witches who ate their guests rose up in her mind. Michaela inched back at the menacing glow in her hostess's eyes.

Kanka gazed longingly toward the entrance. "Your bear has made a kill. If he hurries, the blood will still be warm when he returns."

She did not ask how Kanka knew. The sorceress was already on her feet, tugging on her thick mukluks over her bare hands.

"Come, child. He is traveling fast."

Michaela pulled on the great heavy parka and thick gloves, drawing up the hood as she followed Kanka out into the cold. The sun was still up, hovering the same distance over the horizon. How could that be? she wondered as she realized it was not in the same place at all. It had moved to the northern sky, as if circling them.

Her mind furnished the answer. Summer in the far north, the sun never set.

"There!" Kanka pointed.

She followed the direction of the sorceress's arm and saw a brown mass moving closer. After several minutes she could make out Sebastian, running upright with something big slung across his shoulders. As he neared, she recognized it was a huge musk ox. Great snowballs of ice bounced like beads from the carcass's shaggy coat, and its giant head lolled in time with Sebastian's running stride.

"Is it still warm?" Kanka sounded so hopeful, Michaela could not repress a shudder.

Sebastian dropped the kill at Kanka's feet and she threw her high gloves to the ground. Michaela gasped as she realized Kanka's hands had coiled into vicious-looking talons. Her nails were not that long a moment ago.

The sorceress gave a delighted shriek and pitched forward. Michaela recalled the power with which the sorceress had crushed the vertebra of a whale and staggered back.

There was a renting sound as she tore into the abdomen with her bare hands, spilling the bloody innards on the blue ice. She tore at the liver, lifting the glistening treasure to her lips.

Michaela could not stifle a cry of horror as Kanka's mouth opened unnaturally wide, like a crocodile showing an army of terrible pointed teeth.

It was too much. Michaela ran back into the shelter made of the bones of whales. Behind her she heard the sound of tearing cartilage and cracking bone.

Sebastian followed her, catching up and dragging her forward until he held her against his wide, warm chest.

"No!" she howled.

His hands dropped away and she scrambled to the fire. He stood there staring at her with a look of such sorrow. Her fear began to melt.

His face flushed. "I could not leave you to die. I am sorry, Michaela. I never knew you were Niyanoka."

She came to her senses then. He was not a savage creature like Kanka. He had a heart and he had a mind. He had done everything, even jeopardizing his life to keep her safe. And she repaid him by running.

He reached for her, and she stared down at the hands that had stroked her and teased her until she melted in his embrace. Nothing had changed—everything had changed.

"I won't hurt you," he said.

She stood trembling before him. "I know."

"And I will take you to your people. Once you are safe, I will leave you. But don't look at me like that. I can't abide it."

She dropped her gaze to the green flames as she

struggled to hold back her tears. Slowly, she inched closer, looping her arms around his ribs and resting her head on his chest, drawing comfort from the steady drumbeat of his heart. Half-animal, that's what Kanka had said. Michaela did not understand it, but knew what was in her own heart.

"I don't want you to leave me."

He grunted. "Because you are afraid. Once you meet your kind, once you feel safe, you will feel differently." He did not add the rest—that once she met them, she would want him no longer.

He stood stiffly, resisting the need to hold her until the yearning overtook him. How he wanted her in his world.

But she was a Spirit Child. Regardless of her feelings, her people would drive him off. It had been so since the war, since his people tried to protect the animals by killing the men. His ancestors had started with the protectors of men and many of her kind were killed.

Her voice was velvet. "I *am* afraid, but it's not the only reason I want you to stay."

He drew back, pushing her gently to arm's length. "Michaela, your people and my people, they do not mix. You have been raised by humans, so you do not understand how things are."

"Kanka told me all that and I don't care." She stared earnestly up at him, her lovely eyes wide and sincere. "I love you, Sebastian."

Oh, his heart was bursting. How he had longed to hear these words from her, but not now when there was no hope.

"No." It was impossible. He could not consider it, even for one heartbeat, for if he did…if he did. She did not understand the ways of her people. They would never accept her if she broke their laws. And she needed the Niyanoka to protect her from Nagi. He must think of what was best for her.

"What do you mean, no? I love you. I know what you are and it makes no difference."

He gripped her arms and noted the change. She was no longer under Nagi's control. Kanka had succeeded in freeing her of the Spirit Wound. There was nothing now that he could do for her, except lead her to her people.

"It does, little rabbit. You cannot choose one such as me. Your people will not allow it."

"Then I won't go to them."

"You must."

Her eyes brimmed with tears now. The sight made his stomach constrict. He never meant to cause her pain.

"Why must I?" she whispered.

"Because they can teach you how to fight Nagi."

"Like they taught my father? Nagi still killed him."

Now he understood. She might think this feeling was love, but it was not. He had successfully defended her, and she saw him as her only hope.

It did not make him feel better to know this. Possibly she did not even recognize the truth herself.

"You don't love me," he said, wishing he could pull her close and feel her soft curves mold to him.

"I do. Why don't you believe me?"

"Because I see things you do not."

"What can I say to convince you, Sebastian?"

He shook his head. Humans needed words. An animal proved devotion through deeds. And that was why he would take her to the Niyanoka and then he would give her up.

Chapter 20

Kanka's voice rang with satisfaction as she cleared the entrance. "A fine tribute, bear!"

The old woman rubbed snow on her face to remove the stain of blood. Pink ice fell from her long, pale fingers. Her lips now curled in a natural smile, as benign as any grandmother's. But Michaela was not fooled. She had seen Kanka eat and would be forever cautious.

"I left the skull. Excellent horns on that one."

Michaela's eyes widened in astonishment as she realized the sorceress had eaten the entire ox.

"Time to bring her powers, I think."

Sebastian looked glummer than she had ever seen him. Would this transformation change her heart?

"Wait," said Michaela. "I don't want to change."

Kanka's brows rose as she registered surprise. "You choose death?"

Michaela opened her mouth but found her voice had deserted her.

Kanka nodded her head in understanding. "Nagi, he try to kill you early, before you had your powers. Might still, but at least this way you have a chance. Strip off that coat and boots."

Michaela stared at Sebastian.

"Do you think he can keep you safe?" She made a dismissive sound through her lips. "Come now."

Michaela complied.

"Lie down by my fire."

She didn't want to. "Can I stand?"

Kanka laughed. "You can. But when your powers come they'll knock you to the ground. Best be on the ground already." She tapped the solid ice with the toe of her boot. "Your choice."

Michaela's heart hammered in terror over what would happen next. Sebastian extended his hand, and she latched on to it with both of hers. He led her to a large fur that looked much like the musk ox she had seen a few moments ago.

"Lie down, rabbit. I'll be here."

His gentle voice gave her the strength she needed to take her place. She folded onto the fur and then reclined. Sebastian sat at her side as Kanka crept near.

Kanka lifted a hand and then noted the blood there.

"Honestly," she muttered, and thrust her hands into the green flames. There was a hiss as the blood burned to dust and fell away, leaving her flesh untouched.

Kanka regarded her hand before turning back to Michaela. "When the powers come, they come all at once. Make you sick, likely. My magic don't bring the pain. That comes from breaking your father's magic and the surge of your gifts. Be like the river ice breakup—sudden, violent." She met Michaela's eyes. "You'll see things differently after that."

Michaela opened her mouth to protest.

Kanka glared. "They come in two years, anyway. But you won't live to see that day."

She closed her mouth. Kanka reached into the flames again, delving into her green coals, scooping a handful, then held them over Michaela as if she grasped a handful of potting soil instead of burning embers. Her pewter eyes closed and she began to chant.

Michaela shrank into the fur in a futile attempt to stop this. Sebastian's hand pressed her down to the hide and she grasped his wrist, staring up at his taut face and anxious eyes.

He was afraid. It was all she needed to send her scrambling to escape, but Sebastian was too strong and he held her in place.

Kanka clapped her hands together, crushing the embers into tiny specks of glowing green light that fell in a meteor shower over Michaela, burning through clothing. Each one landed with a tiny electric shock. She writhed under the assault. The embers smoldered on her skin with an eerie luminosity. A tsunami of nausea threw her back, and she arched as every muscle fiber corded. She thought her tendons would tear from the bones, and she screamed in anguish. Next her body jerked like a rat shaken in the mouth of a terrier. Pinpricks of light exploded before her eyes and she thought she would pass out, but the jolting ceased, settling into an unaccustomed tingling. It was not an unpleasant sensation, this feeling, as if someone swept her skin with a soft hairbrush. She glanced down to see the greenish glow fading.

She tried to speak, but her voice would not work.

"Rest," commanded Kanka.

Sebastian stroked her forehead, but she could not keep her eyes open. It was as if Kanka's order could not be disobeyed. She fought, but her traitorous eyelids dropped closed.

She flowed on gentle waves in a warm sea. Was this real or did she dream? She bobbed along, staring at the blue sky. Gradually, the summer blue changed to gray and then to the crystalline blue of glacial ice. She blinked up at the ceiling of Kanka's hut, recognizing the crisscrossing jawbones of great whales.

Had Kanka eaten them whole as well?

"She's waking," said the sorceress.

Sebastian's face loomed, his brow etched in concern. Michaela had her powers now, but nothing had changed. She wanted to tell him so but could not speak.

"Shh. Give yourself a moment to wake."

Kanka held a cup to her lips and Sebastian lifted her head. Why couldn't she lift her own head?

"Drink."

She did, finding it hard to swallow.

She shifted and had to clench her teeth at the ache in

her joints. Someone had draped several heavy hides over her in the time she had been unconscious. This stiffness reminded her of the coma. Her body had failed to obey her commands then, as well. Her heartbeat quickened as possibilities stirred.

Sebastian eased her to a sitting position.

"How long have I slept?"

Sebastian glanced at the sorceress, deferring to her.

"By your measure of time, one month."

"One month!" She threw up her arms. "That's impossible. I would have died."

"You are a Halfling. You can go without food a long time now. And you will live perhaps three hundred years if you are lucky."

"Three..." Michaela gripped her forehead with both hands at this bit of information. She looked to Sebastian, recalling he was already one hundred, by Kanka's account. "How long do you live?"

"Two to four hundred seasons. It depends."

"On what?"

He looked away.

Michaela did the math in her head. She might outlive him by as much as two hundred years. That notion hurt her in a place she never felt before. But he might live another three, with her, if she could only convince him to stay.

"She is well now and stronger even than she knows," said Kanka. "Take her to her people, bear, and then go back to your wild places."

Sebastian stood stiffly. She noted how skinny he looked.

"Did you wait by me while I slept?" Michaela asked.

He nodded.

His devotion warmed her, giving her hope that he might share her feelings, after all. She clasped his hand and felt him tense. The uncertainty grew inside her.

Kanka drew on her parka and headed outside. Sebastian helped Michaela change back into her old clothing, then guided her as she tottered on unsteady legs. Outside she saw the frozen skull of the musk ox adorning the rib of a whale. She repressed a shiver as she stepped past the evidence of Kanka's appetite.

"Move off. Don't want those blundering birds near my lovely bones."

Sebastian lifted his arms and glanced toward the overcast skies.

"They don't fly well this far north. Too cold for thunder," said Kanka.

The distant crack and boom belied her admonition.

"Except in the summer," she amended.

Michaela gripped Sebastian tight and then remembered her manners. "Thank you, Kanka. I am in your debt."

Kanka gave a wolfish smile. "Remember that when I seek payment."

Michaela quaked at the possibilities. It was like swearing an oath to the Godfather. Kanka could make any number of offers that she would be unable to refuse.

"Goodbye, Bear. Remember to follow your instincts."

Sebastian glanced from the sky and scowled as if he did not need reminding to do what he had always done.

The vortex formed above them. This time Michaela

anticipated it. Perhaps she would see the Thunderbeings this time.

They lifted from the ground to the rumble of their mighty hooves. Michaela stared hard into the swirling wind, catching glimpses of long striding legs and powerful arching necks. They were mighty, these steeds of the sky.

She drew a sigh in admiration and recognized she breathed without difficulty. Sebastian glanced down at her and smiled. She grinned at him in return as they flew in the arms of the Thunderbeings.

They landed with a thud, as if their hosts wished them to recall they could not fly without their benevolence. Michaela wobbled, but Sebastian held her as he called his thanks to the heavens.

It was dark here, except for the glow of streetlamps lining the sidewalk. Cars and SUVs were parked closely and the buildings looked like warehouses, with metal gates closed and locked for the night.

"Where are we?"

"Seattle."

Michaela's first thought was that she didn't have her passport. She gave a rueful smile. That was certainly the least of her worries.

"Why here?"

"It's near the House of Spirits, a wine-and-coffee bar."

Michaela wrinkled her brow, wondering what the heck coffee bars had to do with Nagi.

"They have an open microphone on Thursdays for poetry and philosophy."

"Is it Thursday?"

"No idea. The point is, it's very Niyanoka, discussing stuff like that while they drink flavored coffee out of pretty cups."

He sounded disgruntled.

"I like pretty cups."

He frowned. "Of course you do."

Somehow she felt her admission had let him down.

"It is owned by a family of Niyanoka and many of the customers are also of your kind. They are the only Niyanoka I know of."

"They live in Seattle?"

"There are many more in Scottsdale, some in Boulder, but I do not know where. They favor places where the earth energy is strong. I hear they like Herkimer in New York, though I have never been to those low hills."

She turned to him, surprised to see his hair drawn neatly back from his face. He wore a blue oxford shirt, khakis and Docksiders without socks. Only his necklace remained unchanged.

"You never take it off?" She motioned to the turquoise.

"No. It is a part of me, my coat when in human form. I wear it to keep it safe, but can change its appearance." He waved a hand over the pendant, and he now wore a gold chain with a medicine wheel charm.

"I prefer the other." Michaela stared down at her clothing. She still wore her tattered camisole, worn blue jeans and sealskin boots. "I wish I could do that."

Sebastian looped an arm over her shoulders. "You have other gifts."

"You can't change my clothes, can you?"

"Afraid not."

Michaela sighed and brushed the dirt from her jeans and fingered the ragged fringe of lace at her hips.

They walked past a warehouse ringed in a fence topped with razor wire and continued ten long blocks, past brick industrial buildings and along sidewalks that glistened from an earlier rain, before seeing another soul. Finally, she saw a group of unsavory characters loitering by the closed garage door of an auto repair shop tagged with graffiti. These men with no destination seemed to claim ownership of this patch of pavement. The largest lifted his head, assessing his prey, then took one step in their direction as the others swept out behind him in a classic attack formation. A battered fedora shaded the leader's eyes, but the smile was clear, a wicked little slash that said he thought he was in charge.

Sebastian's smile was broader and caused his opponent to hesitate, the corners of his mouth descending.

"Got a light?"

Michaela tried to step around the guy without making eye contact, but Sebastian halted her with one hand. He extended the other with such force that the man before her shot into the air, as a tearing sound mingled with his scream. The ragged remains of a green T-shirt dangled from Sebastian's clenched fist. The man hit the sidewalk ten feet back, a row of gashes bleeding on his chest.

His fellows backed away, hands raised.

"Pity," muttered Sebastian as they abandoned their writhing friend in favor of retreat. He looped his arm through hers and set them in motion.

"You could have killed him," she whispered.

"If I chose to." He glanced back. "Were there any ghosts?"

"What?"

"Hanging about them?"

She craned her neck. "I didn't see any."

"Then they haven't killed yet. But they will."

The neighborhood began to change. A laundromat appeared first and beside it a check-cashing place, now gated and locked. Just beyond, two bars nestled side by side as if trying to keep each other company. Next came a deli, the metal bars now drawn down over the entrance. Someone had tagged the brick surface just beyond with green spray paint.

The next block looked more hopeful. Trees grew from neat squares of dirt cut from the pavement, flanked by a series of shops, all closed. Ahead a well-lit establishment with outdoor tables glowed with flickering oil lamps and strings of white lights like a welcoming port. On each table sat little vases of black-eyed Susans. Potted palms flanked the gap in the low wrought-iron fence encircling the outdoor tables of the eatery. Palm fronds glistened with raindrops as customers sat enclosed in this oasis of civility.

A rail-thin waitress slipped between two tables carrying a small tray holding two steaming cups. She had a tattoo of a sun low in the center of her back and her hot-pink T-shirt was so tight it rode up to her ribs.

Michaela inhaled the inviting scent of brewing coffee. Then she sensed something. It was like nothing she'd ever experienced before, like a little pinprick on her skin.

"What was that?"

Sebastian paused scenting the air. "What?"

Michaela moved toward the café and halted. Twenty paces away a pretty brunette sat at the last table with her back to the other customers. Before her sat a cup of coffee and an untouched biscotti. She read from a dog-eared novel, while across from her sat a young man who was entirely transparent. He cradled his chin in his hand, elbow propped on the table as he gazed longingly at the woman.

"Sebastian. I can see right through him," she whispered.

He looked around. "Who?"

Chapter 21

Michaela lifted a finger to chest level, keeping her arm tucked close to her body so as not to draw attention. "That man, that ghost-man, sitting right there."

Sebastian took a step closer, cocking his head and inhaling deeply. She knew he used his most powerful perceptions, his hearing and his sense of smell.

"The cookie has cinnamon in it, the coffee is sweetened with raw sugar and the woman is wearing a scent of musk, but I sense nothing else."

She wiggled her finger. "But he's there."

Sebastian gave her a long look. "A ghost. You can see them now. What is it doing?"

"Just watching the woman."

"He waits for his mate, then. His choice."

Michaela glanced back to see the man now staring at her; he rose from his seat. She pressed closer to Sebastian and he ushered her toward the entrance.

A crash of crockery colliding with concrete came from their left. Michaela jumped, turning to find a second waitress staring at them with slack-jawed amazement as her abandoned serving tray spun in a noisy circle at her feet.

Michaela clamped her hands over her tingling ears. "Sebastian, what is that?"

Sebastian gripped her shoulders and stared at her. "What?"

"My ears are hot."

"Perhaps a signal that you are in the presence of another Niyanoka." He motioned with his chin toward the waitress with the bangs fringed in royal blue.

Michaela recalled Kanka saying something about now being able to recognize Supernaturals.

The waitress stormed forward, speaking to Sebastian. "Just what do you think you're doing?"

Michaela cowered at the obvious fury in her face. She was positively scarlet and a golden circle of light surrounded her. What the heck was that?

"Let go of her, Skinwalker."

Sebastian's hand dropped from Michaela's shoulders as he faced the woman. "She had no knowledge of what she is until Kanka restored her powers."

The woman's mouth dropped open again. She straightened, reassessing Sebastian. The woman reached out for Michaela. "Come on."

Michaela inched closer to Sebastian.

"Go on," he coaxed. But his expression remained tight.

"Are you coming?" Michaela whispered.

"He's not welcome here," said the waitress, dropping a proprietary arm around Michaela's shoulders.

Michaela shook her off. "Let go of me."

The waitress glanced around, then leaned forward and hissed, "But you belong with us."

Michaela set her jaw and stared at Sebastian. "You promised not to leave me while Nagi is still a threat."

"Nagi?" The fear in the waitress's voice was apparent. She dropped her voice and glanced at the gawking customers. She motioned with her head. "Over here."

They followed her down the street past the greenery and tidy fencing. Then she rounded on them both.

"What has Nagi to do with you?"

Michaela's fright had now dissolved, replaced by a scalding dislike for this woman. She drew herself up.

"He attacked me and my 'people' did not rescue me." Michaela pointed at Sebastian. "He did."

The woman rubbed her chin, dragging her index finger thoughtfully over the metal stud set below her bottom lip.

"She is Ghost Clan," said Sebastian.

The waitress's eyes grew round as she stared at Michaela. It seemed forever before she spoke.

"Go down this side street. We'll meet you out back." She glared at Sebastian. "Both of you."

He nodded and led Michaela away.

"I don't like her."

"This is where you belong."

She halted in the alley. "I belong with you. Please, Sebastian."

"Once you understand. You have no history of your kind, no connection. But once you meet them, you will see, you will—"

"Become a snarky little racist like my new friend? No, I won't."

His smile seemed sad and his shoulders drooped in defeat.

"Do you want to be rid of me?" she asked.

He hesitated just long enough for her insides to go cold.

"I want you to be safe."

"You promised not to leave me."

"Until you were safe," he qualified.

"You think little Miss Body Armor can protect me? She's got more studs than a new house."

Her ears were tingling again, stronger this time. She clamped a hand over one as she stared up at Sebastian. "There're more of them."

Three figures appeared at the end of the alley, silhouetted by the floodlight behind the café. Michaela repressed the urge to run as Sebastian placed a firm hand on her lower back, ushering her forward.

The group gave way as she approached, standing close together in a half circle: a man, a woman and the waitress, each glowing with a soft golden light that surrounded them like a cloud.

The woman shook her head in a restless motion that cast her long braid back over her shoulder. The gesture and her long thick bangs reminded Michaela of a Shetland pony.

"Welcome, traveler. I am Narissa and this is my husband, Karl, and you have met my daughter, Michelle."

"Mickey," chirped the girl.

Narissa's face tightened at her daughter's interjection. "We understand you just discovered your gifts. A Seer of Souls. We feared this clan was gone." She turned to Sebastian. "Thank you for bringing her. We will ensure her care. You may go."

They dismissed him like a servant.

Michaela glowered. The woman's benevolent smile ticked Michaela off. "Thank you, but he's staying."

"You do not yet understand our ways."

"Oh, I get the gist."

Karl cleared his throat and spoke in a slow, easy drawl that surprised her. "Then you'll see, I'm sure, that we cannot have him here. It's not done and—" he faced Sebastian with a condescending smile "—and while we are appreciative, if not surprised, at the bear's forbearance, it doesn't change things."

Michaela found the man's Southern honey just as irritating as his wife's condescending air. So Michaela turned to Sebastian. "Why am I here, exactly?"

"To learn to use your skills."

She faced her circle. "Which one of you knows how to train a Seer of Souls?"

No one spoke.

"Your skills are…?"

"My husband can read the minds of children. He works with child-protective services. Michelle and I—"

"Mickey," interjected Michelle.

She cast her a look of disapproval, then settled back into her smug expression. "My daughter and I can walk in the dreams of others."

Michaela thought that sounded creepy. What did they

do in another person's dreams? She recalled Nagi using the same approach with her and her apprehension grew.

"And you will train me to use my power?"

"We will teach you our ways and introduce you to our community, connect you with those who can shelter you from your enemies."

Michaela hesitated. Her heart told her to go with Sebastian. But she wondered if these people could keep her safe from Nagi?

"I'm sorry if my daughter insulted your…companion," drawled Karl. "It is unusual for us to have direct contact with his kind."

"Can you stop Nagi?" asked Michaela.

Narissa looked taken aback. "No one can stop him, but we can discover what he wants."

"He wants me dead."

"Unlikely," said Karl. "It is against natural law for Nagi to come to this plane, except to collect the evil ones who refuse to walk the Way of Souls. He does not pursue the living."

"He attacked me."

Karl held a skeptical expression but extended his hand to her. "We will hold a council to investigate this. In the meantime, you stay with my family."

Narissa motioned toward the golden light flooding from the kitchen door. "Come inside, dear."

Michaela did not move. "And my friend?"

Her voice turned frosty. "He may not enter here."

Michaela lifted her hands in surrender. "Okay. Thanks for the offer. I'll pass. Come on, Sebastian." She turned to go.

"Wait," said Karl. "You cannot stay with him."

Michaela did not give him a second glance. She heard Sebastian follow. As she reached the street, he caught up with her.

"You don't know what you are doing," he said.

"Well, I know what I'm *not* doing—" she thumbed over her shoulder "—staying with them."

He blinked at her. "But they are your people."

"That's my choice, isn't it?"

Sebastian sighed. "No, little rabbit. You are one of them, like it or not."

"Well, I don't like it and I won't stay here." She pressed her hands on her hips, halting to scowl at him.

He took in her expression and matched it with his own grim stare. At last the corner of his mouth quirked.

"It's a mistake."

"So what?"

"I'm not sure, but all actions have consequences. You just bit the hand, you know?"

Michaela flapped her arms in frustration. "Where to now? You want to hail a cab or a tornado?"

"We cannot sleep here because I do not have my plastic and I cannot get funds until tomorrow."

"You have a bank account?"

Sebastian nodded and lifted his brow at her look of utter astonishment. "And a bank. I used to keep my money in gold, but my friend Nicholas is right, metal is heavy and difficult to exchange. Now I have portfolios and real estate. I also have a cattle farm in Alberta, though I much prefer moose and mountain sheep to beef."

Michaela's jaw dropped. "Well, I have some money, but it's back at my cabin."

"We'll go there. It is a place between our worlds."

He led her behind a brick apartment house, where he boosted her over a low fence. They walked in silence down to the docks.

Michacla's eyes widened as she saw a shadow moving along the marina. It pulsed with a red aura.

"There's another," she whispered, pointing. "I can feel its rage." She closed her eyes and saw a man striking him on the head with a full bottle of champagne and then dumping him into the bay. Shc opened her eyes to see the pulsing red shadow hovering out over the water on its way to a houseboat, all aglow on the bay. "He was murdered by the man on that boat."

"Your powers tell you much." Sebastian glanced around. "This looks like a quiet place."

He lifted his arms and called the whirlwind. Michaela gripped him around the middle as they rose. The night was black and moonless, and she could not see the Thunderbirds that swooped in a circle around them. It was a short trip from Seattle to her mother's cabin.

No, not her mother's—her aunt's. Michaela found it hard to internalize this, but she believed Sebastian and Kanka.

Her feet touched down and the winds dispersed. She recognized the slanted birdfeeder first and then the cabin behind it, a mere dark shadow against the trees.

It seemed she had been away for a lifetime.

As she approached the porch, she saw someone rise from the chair. It was her aunt Maggie. But not her aunt.

She was silvery and insubstantial as a spider's web.

"A ghost," she breathed.

"Another one?" said Sebastian, glancing around the clearing.

Michaela pointed to the porch.

"She wants to tell me something, has been trying to tell me something."

Michaela mounted the step, feeling her aunt's love like a warm breeze.

Should have told you about your mom. Mother gave me names of people. Promise to bring you when turned twenty-two. Should have told you. Only wanted you safe.

"I know you did."

Lives in Montana. Cousin of your father. Look behind the volume on medicinal herbs.

"Yes. I'll find it."

Sebastian shifted uncomfortably beside her, staring in the wrong direction.

Father trying to defend you. Mother afraid. Never told me all of it. I only understood on my death. So sorry.

"Don't be. You kept me safe all these years."

Danger stalks you. I'll stay.

"Thank you."

Loved you like my own.

She vanished. Michaela began to cry. Sebastian cradled her in his arms.

"She's staying to watch over me."

"Who?"

"My m-mother, aunt. She's gone now."

He nodded, still looking wary. Michaela drew back and opened the door, which she kept unlocked, flicked on the light and headed straight to the bookshelf, removing one volume. Behind it, she found a little treasure box full of jewelry and a yellowing envelope.

Inside was a slip of paper in an unfamiliar hand. It read: Sally Firehorse, P.O. Box 135, Billings, MT.

Sebastian glanced over her shoulder.

"She's a contact my mother left me. A cousin of my father."

"Your father?"

She nodded.

"A Niyanoka, then."

"A Seer?" Michaela could not keep the hope from her voice.

"Niyanoka only marry others of their kind. Their gifts can come from either parent."

"Kanka said I am the last Seer."

"Then it is so."

Chapter 22

Michaela tried not to let her disappointment bring her low. She was home at last and Sebastian was here with her.

"Are you hungry, rabbit?"

She was. Ravenous, in fact. Her healing stupor had lasted a month, according to Sebastian. She lifted her hands to her cheeks.

Sebastian confirmed her worry. "You have lost weight."

"I should be dead." She dropped her hands. "A month without eating. It's ridiculous."

"I'll make you some soup." He turned toward the dining room.

"Soup? Are you kidding? I'm famished."

"Your stomach is not accustomed to food. Best to begin slowly."

He continued toward the kitchen, leaving her to trail behind. When she caught up, he had the light on and was standing at the butcher's block holding a sheet of paper.

"Who is Ron?"

"He's my mom's boyfriend." She shook her head at the mistake. "I mean my aunt's, or he was."

She glanced at the page, which read: "Michaela, call me, please," followed by the number she knew by heart.

"Oh, he must be worried sick." She grabbed the phone off the cradle and paused.

What would she say—that she had been attacked by a bear, rescued by a Skinwalker and was just returning from visiting a sorceress with Nagi hot on her trail?

She lowered the handset to its place and glanced at the microwave clock. It read 2:00 a.m.

She felt a moment's relief. "Too late to call."

Sebastian found a can of chicken soup and the can opener while she rummaged in the drawers retrieving an unopened bag of oyster crackers. In a few minutes the meager meal was ready.

They sat side by side at the kitchen table. Michaela leaned forward to inhaled the aroma of the soup. Her stomach roused and grumbled long and insistently. Sebastian laughed.

"Now *you* sound like a bear."

"That's my clan." She lifted her spoon. It teetered as she recalled she was also of the Ghost Clan, the last of the Ghost Clan.

She had nearly drained the contents of her bowl when she noticed he was not eating. She held her spoon between the bowl and her mouth, a noodle dangling precariously from the silverware. He was staring out the black window.

She craned her neck, fearing Nagi. "What's wrong?"

"I was wondering about Bess. It's been over a month since I saw her. I thought she'd be back by now."

She lowered the spoon and stared quizzically at him. "How would she know where we are?" Her eyes rounded as pieces fell into place. "She doesn't have a cabin tucked up in the woods behind yours, does she?"

Sebastian shook his head.

Michaela thought back and gasped. "She's Inanoka!"

He nodded.

She slumped back in her stool. But of course it made sense. She appeared from nowhere. The way she walked, dressed and spoke were all odd.

"I can't believe it." She rubbed her mouth with the napkin then met his gaze. "A raven. She can fly?"

"Beautifully."

Michaela felt sick at her suspicions at the compliment. She fiddled with her spoon, her appetite lost. "Sebastian, are you and she…"

"No, never. Bess isn't fond of me, or at least not in that way. But what you are asking is if I have ever been in love."

He was so direct, it startled her to speechlessness.

"I was, and I also once took a bride."

She sat back in her chair and listened as he told of the young bride, not long dead, who had captured his heart and then rejected him. Michaela's heart broke in sympathy for a man who came to believe he was a man no longer.

Sebastian's hand was balled in a fist beside his half-finished soup. She reached for him, but he drew back, escaping her attempt at comfort.

After a few moments he glanced up.

"I'm not that woman, Sebastian."

He nodded, as if suddenly exhausted. Michaela rose and cleared the table, leaving the dishes for the morning.

"Come on," she said, and walked to the threshold.

He rose wearily and followed. "Are you ready to sleep now?"

She had other plans. "Nearly. But I want a shower first. How does that sound?"

"I will wait for you here."

She lowered her chin in a show of stubbornness and irritation. Two could play at this game.

"Fine." She left him there.

In the bathroom she stripped off her clothing, determining to burn them at the first opportunity. Then she set out two clean, fluffy towels and turned on the taps.

Michaela stepped from the soft threads of the looped bath rug and into the hot stream of water, pausing to groan with pleasure. The only thing better would be to have Sebastian here to wash her back. She lathered her body and shampooed her hair as she considered her options. A scream would bring him but she didn't want to be the boy that cried wolf.

She settled for just calling his name. If there was a hint of urgency and alarm in her tone, well, so be it.

"Sebastian!"

There came the sound of running feet. She drew back the curtain. The door crashed open as he charged into the room. His eyes flew around, looking for any threat, and then found it in her eyes.

"What game is this?" he asked.

"A very old one."

He frowned but did not retreat. Instead, he stepped forward to face her. "Niyanoka do not seduce Skin-walkers. It is not done."

"Sue me."

"You do not know what you are doing."

"So you keep telling me." She leaned back, arching, and let the hot water run down her body. Soap bubbles slithered over curves. She opened her eyes and saw she had caught herself a bear.

He stood naked before her, his erection thick and hard.

She stepped back and offered the water stream. "I'll wash you."

"Remember that I tried to do the right thing," he said.

"Certainly."

He stepped in before her, his hands greedy for her as she lathered his wonderful, wide chest. Thick coarse hair and taut muscle played beneath her questing fingers.

The raw need brought her to stillness and the soap slipped from her fingers. She ran her hands down the ribbed muscles of his stomach, causing his erection to twitch.

Desire built in her, rising, beating. This ache, it changed her anticipation into a furious blinding red desire, gripping her so fiercely that she could not move.

"Michaela, what is it? What is wrong?"

She glanced up at him, seeing the taut, straining face and feeling his control slipping as he held her.

"I can feel it now," she whispered.

"What?"

"Your need."

His eyes widened in understanding.

Up until this moment he could read her desires, emotions and thoughts. But now, somehow, the road had become a two-lane highway.

"She brought your powers," he whispered. "Can you really know what I am thinking?"

She closed her eyes and gasped as an image of her riding on top of him, there on the bathroom rug, rose in her mind. Her eyes popped open and she glanced at the four-by-six rug.

Sebastian dragged her to him, pressing his long, hard body to her pliant one. She rocked her hips from side to side, brushing his erection with her belly. It twitched and she felt his surge of pleasure fire inside herself.

Hot water pounded across his shoulders, and she felt that, as well. Their bodies slipped together, skin sliding over wet skin, in a luscious, sensual dance. He spun her in his arms so her bottom locked to his hips. The spray now beat across her chest as she lay her head back against his chest. His hands cupped her breasts, kneading, stroking and driving her mad.

He kissed her neck and shoulder, and she felt the texture of her slick skin in his mouth and the aching pressure of his palms rolling her nipples into hard buds. She rubbed her backside against him and was rewarded by his groan and the hot flare of sensation he felt as her flesh glided over the underside of his erection.

She faced him, dipping momentarily so the water

cascaded over her as she reached for his cock, curious to know what she did to him, fascinated and aroused to experience her fingers stroking him.

The moment she wrapped her hands around him, she found his thoughts trying to control his want. He clenched his teeth and gripped her shoulders, his mind telling her she went too far, telling her that he felt the slick readiness between her legs even as she felt it. Her mind filled with all the things he wanted to do to her and her hand slipped away.

He stepped out of the tub, carrying her backward to the floor in a slow-motion fall. Her back collided with the cushion of the floor mat and he continued to drive her back, forcing her thighs apart with one insistent push of a muscular leg.

She reached for him again, but he captured her wrists, pinning them over her head.

"Enough mischief," he rasped, and positioned himself above her.

She lifted her head, hands still pinned, and saw his glorious erection positioned between her legs. Anticipation surged and she splayed her thighs in invitation. In the next instant he drove into her with enough force to send them both back several inches across the mat. The doubling of the contact brought her to near climax and she cried out his name.

The sight of him, combined with the sensation of his skin gliding into her tight passage, was the most erotic sight of her life. She felt him and she felt his pleasure as he rocked forward to lock them together.

Her body quickened, her release gathering like the

ticking of a time bomb. Her gaze flew to his as she wondered if she could wait the few moments it would take him to reach his pleasure. He had been fighting so hard not to come, and now she was falling over the edge without him.

His gaze locked to hers, and she knew he understood, needed them to experience their orgasm together. His thrusting lost all caution and restraint as again and again he pushed into her. He was close, but the movement was too much and it pushed her over the precipice.

"Oh!" she cried. "Not yet."

"Yes," he growled.

And she felt his seed, still inside his body as it rushed forward with his release. She cried out as his pleasure and hers combined. For a moment she was mindless with the glory of that instant mutual ecstasy. All too soon the waves of satisfaction rippled away.

He fell like a collapsing tree, rolling to her side onto the cold tile. She gasped at the feel of the porcelain on his skin as he dragged her up onto his body, wrapping his strong arms around her.

She closed her eyes and wept at the power and perfection of their joining.

She did not know she had dozed until he sat up, carrying her with him onto his lap. She roused, glancing around. A puddle of water surrounded them on the floor and the shower spewed water into the tub.

She blinked at Sebastian, who guided them to their feet. He grabbed a plush towel and draped it around her shoulders. The knuckles of his fist pressed against her sternum.

He smiled at her, but his thoughts were dark.

What torture to know you possessed exactly what you want and that you will never keep it.

"Never keep what?"

He released the towel as if it burned him and backed away, breaking the contact between them.

He turned his back to her to flip off the water. Then he retrieved a towel and wrapped it low around his hips.

He did not like this invasion of his mind and began to understand why Michaela had been so upset when he had used it to give her pleasure the first time they had coupled.

The towel now covering his lower half, he turned to face her, thankful that she had wrapped her towel tight around her body, covering her from the damp tops of her breasts to the top of her thighs. Her lovely, long legs still glistened with water. He lifted his gaze to her eyes.

"Dry your hair, rabbit, so you don't catch a chill."

She glared at him as he moved past her.

"Where are you going?"

He didn't know. Getting away from her was all he could think to do, away from her glower and stubborn refusal to accept what must be.

He didn't care about the Niyanoka and their silly laws. Not for himself, anyway. But he could not allow her to make such an uninformed decision. She did not understand that she would need them and that by choosing him, she would lose that community.

It was wrong to let her make such a misstep before she fully understood what it would cost her.

He glanced back at her and then withdrew.

Chapter 23

Michaela fumed and then shivered. Finally, she grabbed a second towel and gave her hair a vigorous rub. A glance in the mirror brought her attention to the sagging, sodden bandage around her arm. Her mind shifted from her troubles with Sebastian to her troubles with Nagi.

She dropped the towel and peeled away the leather pad, gaping at what she saw. The injury had completely healed. Michaela wiped away the zinc oxide and stared at the scar that more resembled a finely drawn blue-black tattoo of a medicine wheel than the raised puckering red line she anticipated. How odd. She recalled Kanka's stitches, but somehow they had fused with her skin. Michaela swept her fingers over the marks. They felt smooth and perfect, her sensation had returned and the ghastly gray pigment had disappeared. She was truly healed.

Except for the tear to her Spirit. She shivered.

The fluffy white towel did not fully remove the chill that ran deeper than her pimply gooseflesh. How would she heal the tear?

Michaela headed to her bedroom, changed into her short flannel nightie and strode to the window, drawing back the curtains. Somehow she knew that Sebastian was out there, in the night. She lifted the sashing and leaned over the porch roof.

"If you are out there, come to bed," she called.

She waited but received no reply, so she lowered the window and flipped back the covers. The last time she had been here, she had been anxious to flee her room, running from the threat she did not understand. Now she did and truth was far worse that she had ever imagined. The threat was real. She was hunted by Nagi.

Sebastian was not here to protect her.

She drew on her robe and left the room. Nagi would not find her this night. Perhaps Niyanoka could do without sleep as well as food. Anyway, she was determined to try.

Back in the living room, she glanced toward the porch, catching movement. Her aunt? Sebastian?

There he was, rocking in her aunt's favorite chair. She opened the door, leaning against the jamb.

"Can't sleep?" he asked.

"Not without you."

"You are still under my protection. You don't have to take me to your bed."

"Stop pouting and come to bed."

His jaw dropped. "Bears don't pout."

She grinned and untied her robe, holding it open as she closed the distance between them. When she got within arm's length, he grasped her waist and dragged her into his lap.

She looped her arms around his neck and kissed him, feeling his desire flare with hers. Her low moan encouraged him as his fingers delved beneath the hem of her nightie.

Sebastian didn't carry her to bed until just before dawn and the sun had turned the walls of her room pink before she closed her eyes, but when she did, she was smiling.

Michaela woke to an empty bed. This was getting annoying. Every time she let down her guard, he slipped away.

She dragged on white lace underwear, a matching bra, a soft moss-colored corduroy blouse and tight faded jeans. She paused to drag a comb through the tangle of her hair, and then stooped to find her moccasin slippers under the bed.

"Time to hunt some bear."

A few moments later she entered the kitchen, shivering slightly as she turned on the kettle. A glance out the window found Sebastian talking to a raven, which sat on top of the birdfeeder.

Bess had arrived.

Michaela tried to pretend this was normal as she stepped onto the porch.

"Kettle's on, Bess. Would you like some breakfast?"

Bess hopped down to the grass and took one step before rising from the ground like a dancer unfolding. In human form, she wore a crisp linen skirt with black buttons descending the front, like a string of gleaming raven eyes. Her blouse was low-cut and flirty, to show her cleavage. The fabric cinched her ribs, then fell free in wispy triangles of cloth that reminded Michaela of wings.

"Love some," she said.

Sebastian trailed them.

Bess kissed Michaela on both cheeks. "I'm glad to see you are feeling better."

Michaela pressed both hands over her heart. "You can see it?"

"I can."

"I feel well."

"That is good."

Michaela would have liked a confirmation, but Bess only smiled benevolently. So Michaela motioned to the door and Bess preceded her inside. They made their way to the kitchen, where Michaela started the coffeemaker, poured water from the kettle for Bess's tea and set out the orange juice. When she glanced at the clock, she realized it was past time for lunch.

Sebastian found bacon and eggs and nudged her out of the way so he could cook. She grabbed a cup of coffee before settling beside Bess, who dunked a bag of herbal tea into the hot water and set the mug aside.

"Sebastian filled you in on our adventures?" asked Michaela.

"I understand you are Niyanoka."

"So they tell me."

"I'll try not to hold it against you." Bess winked at her. "And the last Seer of Souls. You see all ghosts?"

"Three so far."

"And they speak to you?" Bess look fascinated and cautious all at once.

Michaela nodded.

"I can talk only to the ones who have crossed and I can see the auras only of the living."

Michaela stared in astonishment. "That is how you knew I was feeling better?"

Bess nodded and lifted her tea, blowing softly on the steaming surface.

"What color is it?"

"A blending of colors. Most vivid is the purple of fresh lilacs. That shows wisdom. This mixes with turquoise at your head. I wondered when I met you at that odd combination. I'd never seen it before. But if you are the last Seer, well, that explains it. And now you have the golden outer aura of all Niyanoka."

"Wisdom?" Michaela sipped her coffee. "I think you've got the wrong girl."

She looked at Sebastian, cocking her head. "What about his?"

Bess cast him a quick glance as he ladled eggs and bacon onto three plates. "A nice vital male blue this morning." She cast him a knowing glance and then returned her attention to Michaela. "Seems well pleased with himself."

Michaela blushed, using her discomposure as an excuse to gather silverware for the meal. Sebastian set the plates on the counter before them.

For the next few minutes the focus shifted to food. Michaela was again surprised at her appetite. When she looked up from her nearly empty plate, it was to find Bess's attention fixed on her.

"The black is gone from your Spirit Wound. Kanka did well in the healing. But your aura is not well seated. It drifts away from your center. All is not right with you."

Michaela felt better since the healing, but different, a little unfocused and confused. She moved her hands to her lap to disguise her discomposure and then cleared her plate to the sink. Her appetite was quite gone and now her breakfast rolled in her unsettled stomach. When she turned back, she found both Bess and Sebastian staring.

Bess's eyes seemed to pin her in place. "I met your father and mother."

Michaela tottered, landing against the butcher block with a thud. Sebastian caught her elbow and righted her with astonishing speed. She read his disquiet at what Bess would tell her. He knew already, for she had told him in the yard. Her eyes rounded. It took a lot to rattle Sebastian. He must have read her panic at his thoughts, for he instantly withdrew his hand.

Bess's dark eyes turned sympathetic. "Sebastian sent me."

Michaela blinked at her in amazement as she realized what this meant. Bess had crossed over the Spirit Road, seen her parents—and come back. She gaped at her guest with renewed respect.

"Your mother is so worried about you. She wanted you to know she did all she could to defend you. They both did."

"How did she die?"

"Protecting you. Your father was a Seer, like you. He said he was curious about the Spirit Road and followed a friend who had departed. With one foot on the Road and one foot on the earth, he could see both worlds. He knew to go forward was to lose his wife and daughter, lose his place in the living world. So he turned back. But by crossing to that plane too soon, he tore his soul."

"Like me." Michaela's body ached with tension.

Bess nodded. "The journey on the Spirit Road takes the soul from the body, separating them forever. The single step causes a rip, and the scent of a rending soul always interests Nagi."

"He can only see ghosts," said Sebastian.

"Close," said Bess. "He can see any living creature that step into his path, but he can only track a torn soul. It sends him a beacon, like a GPS signal."

"But why should he want to track my dad?"

"Like you, he was a Seer of Souls. That made him a threat."

"It's the other way round," said Michaela.

Bess inclined her head. "Granted, Nagi is powerful. But you can see all his ghosts. None of us can do that."

"I don't understand why this makes me dangerous."

"Neither do I. But clearly Nagi is anxious for you to follow your father along the Spirit Road. So why does he not want anyone on this earth who can see ghosts?"

"He should not attack living beings," said Sebastian.

Bess placed a hand gently on his arm. "Granted, but

not all of us do exactly as we should." Bess glanced from Sebastian to Michaela, and Sebastian shifted uneasily.

Michaela followed Bess's gaze. Sebastian had stepped from his path when he rescued her. One step on the wrong path, just like her father. If such a one as Sebastian could break the rules, how much easier would it be for a true Spirit like Nagi?

"He is hunting me."

Bess gave a curt nod and then drained her tea.

"He killed my father?"

Bess adjusted her plate but did not eat. "Your father made himself easy to find by venturing where he did not belong. He tells me that once he understood that Nagi wanted his life, he tried to protect his family."

"By leaving us," Michaela finished. She now understood why her father had abandoned them. He hadn't, not really. He had done his best to lead Nagi from his wife and child.

"It was a good plan, but they made a mistake. Your father agreed to meet your mother at her insistence. Nagi was watching. He attacked, killing your father and wounding your mother. She died of that wound."

A Spirit Wound like he had given to her, an injury that should have killed her. Her mother had died a terrible death, one that Michaela had been spared, because of Sebastian. Her eyes met his. He gave her a look of such open sympathy she felt her heart break.

Her throat closed as the tears came, and she could not speak. Bess draped an arm around her. She rested her head against the taller woman's shoulder as the grief washed through her, making her weak.

She had lost everyone who loved her, but she had not lost her life, because of these Skinwalkers, who broke the rules, for her.

She drew away, mopping her tears on her sleeve. "Why did he have to attack my mother? She was human and no threat to him."

"She was a threat because she carried a child, your brother, who would have grown to be a Seer like you."

Michaela's heart turned to stone. Hatred like nothing she had ever felt bubbled through her bloodstream like lava. This thing had killed her entire family.

Sebastian stroked her shoulder, bringing her back to her surroundings.

"Why didn't he kill me that day?"

"Because he did not know of your existence. Your parents had taken steps to hide you. Your mother told me that before their meeting, she put you in her sister's care and told her to keep you safe until she returned. She never did."

Realization struck Michaela, making her stomach constrict.

"My aunt didn't know."

"She knew your father could see ghosts. A shaman, she thought. She never knew you were like him, more than human."

Silence settled over the room as Michaela grappled with her family's bloody history.

"Why is he killing Seers?" asked Sebastian.

"Because Seers do not see only Spirits. They also see ghosts. Sebastian and I can see Supernaturals and Spirits, even sense animals possessed by ghosts, but to the rest, we are blind."

"Kanka told me that Nagi is not collecting evil ghosts," said Michaela.

The look Sebastian and Bess exchanged stopped Michaela's breath. The two seemed to momentarily forget her presence as they spoke over her head.

"Not collecting?" Bess whispered to Sebastian. "A Seer would know of their presence, easily unmask them, and a talented one could send them over."

"Where Nagi would release them again," said Sebastian.

"Yes, but not without notice. Hihankara would see them escape the Circle. She could alert the other Spirits."

Sebastian nodded. Michaela had never seen him look so serious. His grim expression was positively terrifying.

"Perhaps," he said, "Nagi tires of his gray existence stewarding evil souls, and wants this world as well."

"No," whispered Bess.

"He has used possession to attack the living."

Bess turned to Sebastian. "What if he plans to take animals, as well?"

Sebastian's roar startled the women.

"No one will believe us," whispered Michaela.

"No human, certainly. But the Inanoka will come to our aid."

"What about the Niyanoka?" asked Bess.

"They won't listen to us," growled Sebastian, the rage echoing in the timbre of his deep voice.

"Can the Inanoka stop him?" asked Michaela, turning from one to the other.

"No," said Bess. Her lack of hesitation was unsettling. "We cannot see them until they take possession and then it is too late."

Michaela wrung her hands. "I'll go to the Niyanoka. Maybe they'll listen to me. Maybe they can stop him."

Bess gave her a look of subdued impatience. "I believe Nagi thinks *you* can stop him. It explains the need to eliminate you before you had your powers."

Bess echoed Kanka's words, sending a chill of apprehension up Michaela's spine.

"I don't know how."

"Yet," said Sebastian.

Michaela felt the cold inside her stomach spreading like ice on a river. How could she stop him? He had such power, a true Spirit, while she was just a Halfling without the knowledge needed to use her gifts.

She stared off out the window at the birds on the feeder. Everything looked so normal, but it wasn't, never would be again.

"Your father sends another message. He fought Nagi and lost, but he came away with knowledge of Nagi's power. He believes you can use this knowledge to protect yourself."

Chapter 24

"What message did my father send?" asked Michaela.

Bess turned to Michaela, resting a hand on either shoulder, and stared into her eyes. "Remember I told you that your father tore his soul? This Spirit Wound left residue. This made him easy to track. You have walked that same trail—twice."

Her stomach dropped as she nodded.

"Your body is healed. But as long as your soul is torn, you will be visible to Nagi."

"Kanka said I must fix it. But I don't know how." Michaela had an image of Wendy stitching Peter Pan's shadow back to his feet and gave a hysterical little laugh.

"It is one of your gifts," insisted Bess. "You can heal tears of the soul."

"But I don't know how to do that yet!"

"If you do not discover how quickly, Nagi will finish what he has started. He cannot afford to wait, for your aura burns brighter by the minute. Your powers are growing."

"What good are they if I don't know how to use them?"

"She needs to go to the Niyanoka," Sebastian grumbled.

"No," said Michaela, reaching out and grasping Sebastian's strong arm. "I want to stay with you."

"I can't give you what you need."

"You've kept him from my dreams. You've safeguarded me when no one else could."

Bess lifted a finger to object. "True. For protection, I can think of none better than Sebastian. But who best to guide you? Not the Dreamwalkers or the Mindwalkers. We Inanoka have been of more help than your own kind. How ironic."

Sebastian's voice displayed his agitation, rumbling like thunder. "They are her only hope. She is different from us. You know it is so."

Bess's smile glimmered with a secret. "Not so different than when you picked her up."

Michaela glanced between the two, trying to decipher what Bess implied.

Sebastian ran his long fingers through the thick hair at his temples. "I did not know she was Niyanoka then."

"And now you do. What has changed?"

"Everything."

"And nothing," she said, turning back to Michaela. "She needs a Seer."

Michaela pressed her lips together in frustration. "But I'm the last one. There's no one to teach me."

Michaela did not like Bess's knowing smile. It sent

a shiver down her spine, and she knew she would not like what came next.

"You know Nagi can walk in dreams. But you have great power there, as well. Perhaps the answer lies in slumber."

Michaela shook her head in denial, unwilling to face her nightmares again. She had not had a single one since Sebastian began sleeping at her side, and she wanted very much never to have one again. "Nagi can find me in my dreams."

"Yes," agreed Bess. "But he is not the only one seeking you. If you are brave, you may find your father there. He is your mentor. The Seer who can teach what you must learn."

"Of course," said Sebastian. His complete acceptance of this showed so clearly upon his face, Michaela began to quake.

If he agreed with Bess, then he would leave her—and Nagi would come.

Michaela scrambled for some way to convince them of the impossibility of this plan. "I thought you said that my father could not leave the Spirit World."

"This is so," said Bess. "But in dreams your worlds may touch."

Michaela had no answer.

Bess inclined her head, staring at Michaela from beneath her glossy brows. "Did you listen when your aunt spoke of the old ways?"

Michaela swallowed back her terror and still had to clear her throat before she could speak. "I never thought it would be important."

"Young ones never do." She turned to Sebastian. "We must be certain there are no creatures in this house that Nagi can use against her. No body for him to possess."

She hated herself for asking, but she could not stop herself. "If he wants me dead, why not send some creature to kill Sebastian to get to me?"

Now Sebastian smiled, a rueful, cocky smile that made Michaela feel safe as a baby lion between its mother's paws.

Bess patted Sebastian's strong shoulder. "What creature could kill a fourteen-hundred-pound grizzly?"

Michaela had to agree. Only a man with a high-caliber gun, and he would have to be very lucky. Grizzlies had been known to continue to charge even after being struck by several bullets. They were incredibly strong and ruthless in the attack.

Michaela glanced at Bess. "What about you? He could hurt you for helping me."

"Me?" Her laugh was merry. "Don't worry, little one. I'm safe enough."

Sebastian stepped to her defense a little too quickly, and Michaela was embarrassed by the jealousy that fired in her like a pistol shot.

"Bess can outfly anything. She's as fast as the wind."

"Eagles?" asked Michaela.

Bess waved a dismissive hand. "Soaring is all they are good for and they're too big to maneuver in the trees. The only way to catch a raven is to catch one sleeping, and we are *very* light sleepers."

Silence fell over the three of them and acceptance

settled over Michaela. They were so brave, these two, helping her fight in a battle that was not their own.

She would try to be brave, as well. Though she did not think she had the courage to face Nagi alone, she must risk that to reach her father. She began to tremble again.

"What if I can't find him?" she whispered.

"You will."

She drew a breath and spoke the truth. "I'm frightened."

"Yes," said Bess. "That is as it should be. Only a Heyoka would march fearlessly to meet the ruler of the Circle of Ghosts. I would not send you, but I see no other way."

Sebastian looked as if he had a toothache. Was it hard to leave her? She hoped so. Resisting the urge to run to him and bury her face in his strong, muscular chest was difficult. He had protected her through all of the nightmares that haunted her, but he could not help her in this.

Nor should he have to. The fight was hers and she would face it alone.

"Yes, I'll do it."

The long summer day droned endlessly by until the sun made its descent. Bess cooked dinner, but no one had much appetite.

Sebastian's dour look did nothing to bolster Michaela's flagging spirits. She felt like a condemned prisoner about to face judgment.

"Maybe some wine," said Michaela.

"No," said Bess. "You must not use drugs of any kind. They will make it easier for him."

Easier, as if killing her wouldn't be simple enough.

Sebastian gathered her hand in his. "He will try to frighten you. But remember, he cannot actually touch you without a body, and in your dreams you have equal power."

"Equal?" What did that mean?

"You can fly. You can change from an owl to a mouse. You can search for your father. Call to him and bring him to you. Do this first."

Bess added her opinion. "It will be a race to see if you can find him before Nagi finds you."

"But Nagi cannot touch me?"

"Not your body," clarified Bess.

Ah, he could only make her go mad, then. What a lovely thought.

"But I can still wake up?"

"Yes, but try to reach your father first," she said, "or you will only have to venture forth a second time."

"I've never really had any control of my dreams. They just sort of happen."

Bess's expression turned sour. "They do not just happen. They are your connection to the Spirit World. Those with training can use this connection for great insight."

Michaela glanced at Sebastian with longing. Beside him she had rested safe. "Why can't he stay with me?"

"He has used his powers to keep your dreams undisturbed," said Bess. "He cannot keep out Nagi without also blocking your father."

"Figures."

Bess rose from the table and cleared the dinner plates returning with only two mugs.

Sebastian rose as if on cue and left the room.

Michaela followed him with her eyes, feeling bereft at his departure.

"He goes to check the house for any intruders. If there is so much as a mouse under the floorboards, Sebastian will know." Bess poured the tea and pressed one cup into Michaela's trembling hand.

"You are very young still, but I think you will do well," said Bess.

"I'm twenty-one." Michaela realized that she sounded offended.

"As a Niyanoka, you will see centuries turn. Twenty-one seasons seems just a moment to me."

Michaela looked at Bess, really looked for the first time. Her dark hair and strong features made her beauty radiant and ageless. "How old are you?"

"Me? Oh, old. Nearly two centuries now."

"And Inanoka live three?"

"Usually. Though there have been those who have lived as long as half a millennium. But that is very rare. Sebastian is young, too."

"Young? I heard him say he was more than a hundred."

"This is so, but he was only fourteen when his powers came and already married. We are not like Niyanoka, whose powers are always with them and must be trained. Ours come in a rush like a butterfly bursting from a cocoon. Sebastian's mother had been converted from the old ways by the missionaries. It is why she named him after a Christian saint. Back then, we were not allowed to even speak our language. She witnessed his change and believed he was possessed. She called him the son of the devil. His tribe had been decimated by alcohol and disease. Those that were left lived on reservations a soulless life back then. Few even remembered that the legends were all based on truth, so Sebastian was cast out by the one woman who should have loved him unconditionally."

Michaela found herself trying to imagine a fourteen-year-old Lakota boy at what…the turn of the last century? The whole thing made her so sad her chest hurt.

"What did he do?"

"Oh, can't you guess?" Bess waited, keeping her gaze fixed on her. "He did what any bear would do. He hibernated that first winter and then his mentor found him. After his training he moved north and west by the season until he found the place he still lives today. He has been a bear most of his life. All his attempts to blend with humans have failed, until he no longer tries. Now he changes when he meets another Inanoka or to conduct business. He has led a lonely life.

"I migrate, so I have known many of our kind. Sebastian, very few. He has never found anyone that made him stay in human form for long—until you."

Michaela did not know what to say to that, but she could not stop the rush of joy and hope that flooded her.

"That is why I say he is young, though you will not find a man with a bigger heart or more desire to please, even if his heart is half-animal. He cares for you very much."

"He told you that?"

Bess shook her head. "But it is true, just the same."

Michaela felt her hopes deflate. She recalled his rejection and curled in around herself to absorb the hurt of Sebastian's words.

"You're wrong, Bess. He doesn't want me. He's told me so."

"Don't believe it."

"He said we cannot be together. That Inanoka and Niyanoka do not mate."

Bess sipped her tea, lifting her head just a fraction before swallowing. Then her bright eyes pinned Michaela. "I have never heard it done. But I believe you two will find a new path."

Michaela wanted to believe it, but she feared more heartbreak. Then she recalled something.

She repeated the words that had made no sense until this moment. "Never been, don't mean never will be."

"What?" asked Bess.

"It was something Kanka said to me. I didn't understand it, but…could she have been talking about us?"

Bess's gaze roved about, and Michaela wondered if she read her aura, saw something there.

"She could. As for myself, I have two very good reasons to believe Sebastian will accept you."

She could not keep her voice from relaying her desperation. "What are they? My love for him? Is that what you mean? But then what is the other?"

"I would say your love for him is both reasons. Have faith that your love will make him believe that what is impossible *is* possible."

Michaela clasped Bess's hand. "Thank you. I'm so happy we met."

"You are the first Niyanoka to ever say that. May I give you some advice?"

Michaela nodded, certain that she would speak of Nagi. But instead she gave her these cryptic words.

"Don't keep secrets, not from those you love."

"Secrets?"

Bess smiled and nodded, squeezing her hand before releasing it. "Yes. Simple but important."

Sebastian returned. "There is nothing living here but us."

"Spiders, wasps or anything else that can kill?"

"Nothing."

Bess sighed. "Then we must go."

Michaela felt her knees go watery. She did not want to be alone.

Bess rose from the table and swept to the door in her long graceful strides. Sebastian hesitated.

Michaela wanted to beg Sebastian to stay with her, but more than her fear of Nagi was her fear that he would discover her to be a coward and therefore unworthy of his love. She looked in his eyes and realized her terror was tearing him apart. He could not leave unless she sent him.

She mustered herself, drawing back her shoulders and leveling her chin.

"I'll be fine," she lied. Her voice didn't sound fine. It creaked like an old spring.

Bess hugged Michaela. "We will not go far and we will return with the dawn."

Michaela longed to go with them, but stood stiffly as a soldier on watch.

"Lock the doors and windows." With that, Bess stepped onto the porch, raised one leg to the rail and transformed into a raven lifting into the darkening sky. Her caw signaled her farewell.

Michaela stared in astonishment for a moment before turning to Sebastian. One look at the concern in his worried face and the tears came.

He held her tight. "I wish I could do this thing for you."

So did she, but to say so would be weak, and this man deserved a woman with steel inside her. "I have fought Nagi before I knew what he was. I always woke to escape him. If I cannot find my father, I will do that again."

"Yes. Do."

He stroked her hair and gazed down at her with an expression that looked like love. Bess believed he would accept her and that gave her hope.

"I love you," she whispered.

"Perhaps the man," he said.

Just the man, as if she could not love the beast. Was that the two reasons Bess mentioned? Did he need to know she loved both sides of him?

"The man is a very good kisser. But the bear is better for home defense."

He cocked his head, as if uncertain what to make of her. "Are you teasing me?"

"Trying."

"I will be back before first light, waiting there." He pointed to the center of her yard.

She held him for a moment more and then stepped away. "See you then."

He stepped off the porch and then reached forward,

growing into the mighty bear. He turned to stare at her. She descended the steps, her heart hammering in her chest at what she was about to do.

She walked slowly, overcoming her natural fear with each step, determined to show him that she trusted the bear.

Michaela paused at his mighty head. It was wider than her entire rib cage. Her hand trembled, but she lifted it and rested it gently on the thick fur between his ears. He leaned toward her and groaned as she stroked him, his eyes drifting shut. She leaned forward to whisper in his ear.

"I hope I dream of you."

He shook his mighty head slowly, and then rubbed it against her once before lumbering off. He halted at the tree line and lifted a paw in salute. An instant later he was gone.

Michaela turned back to face her mother's cabin and the longest night of her life.

Chapter 25

Michaela paced, tossed and finally read a book that did not hold her interest. The clock beside her bed ticked away in endless motion, reaching 3:00 a.m. by last check. Soon it would be dawn and her friends would arrive. She could stay awake, had done so on many nights to avoid Nagi. But to do so was just to postpone the inevitable and to disappoint her new friends.

She yawned. She had to do this.

The words began to blur and the book wobbled as she wrestled with consciousness. Her hold on the book slackened as she dozed.

The next moment she walked in an unfamiliar house of menacing, shadowy corners and gray wallpaper. As she entered one room, she realized she carried the pink blanket she dragged everywhere with her as a child. Her mother called it “rags” for obvious reasons, but now it was restored to its former glory—the only bright and hopeful object in this grim reality. She lifted her old friend to her nose, inhaling the comforting scent of fabric softener and detergent.

The tug came unexpectedly as the blanket was ripped from her hand and pulled through the solid door before her. Away went any security she had. She stared at the door, certain a ghost lay behind it.

She thought about the blanket: fuzzy, soft, pink and impossibly new. It was gone long ago, which meant…this was a dream. Bess said she could control her dreams.

Her hand shook as she reached for the door, and she had to stop to clench her fist once before she could find the courage to turn the knob.

She pictured what lay on the other side, and then twisted the handle, throwing open the door.

There before her lay all the stars in the heavens stretched out to infinity, and at the center, connected to her murky door, lay the Milky Way.

She had found the path to the Spirit World. Her gaze traveled up the glittering trail of silver light. Ahead she saw a figure…her father?

It turned. There stood a hunched crone who stared down at her with eyes as black as tar. Hihankara, the guardian of the Spirit Road. She would not let Michaela pass.

She must try. Michaela lifted a foot to take her first step, and then recalled what had happened to her father when he had found this road. She stopped. No, he must come to her. She cupped her hands to her mouth and called into the night sky.

"Father! It is Michaela. Come here."

She did not know what she expected, some silvery vapor of glimmering light, perhaps.

But instead there came a voice from behind her.

"I am here, sweet pea."

She gasped as she recalled the voice and endearment, though she did not even remember that she knew. She whirled and found him there, not much older than she was, definitely less than thirty. Or was he three hundred?

"Daddy!"

She threw herself into his arms and he hugged her, kissing the middle of her forehead in a gesture sweet and hauntingly familiar.

"How is my Dreamchild?"

She glanced up at him with a puzzled look.

"You always had the most power in your dreams. I never suppressed that. I visited you here, when I still had a body. I am glad to see you are…" He paused as he noticed the circular scar on her arm, now a vibrant burgundy color. "He has marked you."

"Yes." She glanced from the scar back to her father. "I need the knowledge of a Seer."

Her father's eyes rounded. "Bess found you."

Michaela nodded. "She sent me."

"Nagi is a formidable foe. We are not strong enough to survive attacks of a Spirit. When facing a superior enemy, it is best to mimic the methods of the weaker creatures of the earth."

"What methods?"

"Concealment. Nagi cannot attack what he cannot see."

"But I have to beat him."

"No, sweet pea. You have to escape him."

"But he keeps finding me."

Her father nodded. "Because of the Spirit Wound. Nagi can only track one whose soul has left their body. That makes it easy to collect the evil ghosts that seek to avoid Hihankara's judgment on the Sky Road."

Michaela glanced back at the open door and saw the old hag creeping closer, as if to eavesdrop. Her face was rough and brown as the thick bark of a redwood, but still Michaela made out the swirling blue tattoos that covered her face and leathery neck.

Michaela looked away, hoping she would not face judgment for many, many years.

"As he killed me, he told me I left a nice trail for him. You leave a trail as well, daughter. If you repair this break, your trail will vanish. Then he will only see you if your paths cross, and I hope you will note him first and go the other way."

"Camouflage," she whispered. "Can you fix the tear?"

He shook his head. "Only you can do so. The power to draw together mind, body and spirit is in every living soul."

"How?"

"All three must all want one thing above all others. It is rare for them to share the same aim. The soul wants enlightenment, while the mind remains mired in minutia and the body, ever ravenous, calls for sustenance and stimulation. But you'll know when you succeed."

"What will happen?"

"You'll feel your soul and body realign." Her father lifted his brow.

"How do I do that?"

"I know only what you must do, not how you must do it."

Her father glanced around as if hearing something she could not. His agitation made her anxious.

"Is there anything else I must know?"

"Much. Once you fix this break, we will visit again. I will be grateful to teach you to use your power and be indebted to your Inanoka, as well, for he gives me grandchildren."

Michaela stared at him. "What?"

"You carry his children—two. A boy and a girl. They will be great Seers, but more than this, I think. Did you know your mother was of the Bear Clan?"

"I'm pregnant?"

He nodded.

"You're sure?"

"I can see these souls as surely as I can see yours."

Michaela glanced down at her stomach in astonishment. The need to survive this ordeal now pulsed in her veins. She had to find the way to protect herself, for that was the only way to protect her children.

She rested a hand on her flat belly as acceptance settled. "Twins."

In that moment, she remembered Bess's prediction. The raven woman said there were two reasons Sebastian would accept her and that both were love. Their children. Michaela's heart ached with the overwhelming joy.

"Your mother will be so pleased."

Her father smiled at her and she felt guilty for all the anger she had held for him, all the years she thought he had abandoned her, when he had only done what she would do to protect her child.

"I'm sorry, Daddy, for not trusting you."

He waved a hand in dismissal. Then the smile dropped from his face and his features grew alert. He placed a hand on her back, ushering her away from the door.

"You must go back now. He is coming and he has more strength in this world than yours."

"Nagi?"

Her father nodded, and she felt a chill cross her heart. She clutched at her belly, fearing now for her life and those she carried.

Her father gave her a hasty kiss and stepped through the open door. He turned to Hihankara. "This is my daughter."

The crone stared. "I sent her back. She doesn't have the proper tattoos."

"Because she is still alive."

"Ah," said the woman.

Her father held the edge of the cracked and peeling door. "Wake up now, sweet pea. Hurry. He's coming."

The door slammed in her face.

The sound of the door banging the frame brought Michaela awake. Was it in her dreams or was someone trying to get in? Sweat beaded on her brow and made the hair at her temples and neck damp. She clutched the sheets to her chest and listened to the silence that filled her room.

She did not question if her dream was real, for she now had complete confidence in the dream world.

Her father's message rang in her mind. Nagi could find her unless she could heal her Spirit.

Cold fear washed her body as she sat up. What had he said, that her mind, soul and body must want something in unison?

Survival—that was what she wanted, but she felt no different than she had since the attack. Her father said she would know if she succeeded, would feel it, so she knew she had not repaired the tear.

She threw off the tangled sheets and stepped from the bed. The moisture on her body cooled, making her shiver. She exchanged her thin cotton nightie for slacks and a lilac-colored turtleneck sweater. She dug a favorite pair of polar fleece socks from beneath the bed and slipped them onto her cold feet before peering out the window at the gray gloom. The overcast skies seemed to keep the dawn at bay. She glanced at her clock. Only five in the morning.

She flipped back the curtain and peered out at the trees' dark silhouettes against the deep blue predawn sky and then located a favorite pair of backless sneakers and slid into them on her way out the door. Nagi had been close, but she had evaded him by waking.

How long until dawn? It embarrassed her how much she longed for Sebastian to be here with her. She did not feel safe without him. No, it was not fear she felt but loneliness—the ache that comes from missing one you love. She knew the difference between need and love, even if Sebastian though she confused the two. She would have to make him believe her.

Another thought stole into her mind. She was to be a mother.

She cradled her stomach in wonder. "Shall we get some breakfast?"

Hunger now held her occupied as she made her way to the kitchen. The dawn now made it possible to see the yard, but the window turned black as soon as she flipped on the light. She pressed down her anticipation. Sebastian would be here soon. In the meantime, she drew out the makings for pancakes.

"No blueberries this time!" She stood with her back to the window as she stirred the batter, trying to pretend that the reflective surface did not disconcert her.

Would their babies have their father's gifts?

The sound of loose gravel crunching under tires reached her, and she placed the bowl aside so she could peer out the window. Outside, she spied a familiar rusty red pickup truck, recognizing it immediately.

Ron—her mother's boyfriend, who had been there to help her with her mother's things and the countless other details that follow the death of a loved one. No, wait, her aunt's boyfriend. This was so confusing.

She rinsed her hands as the brake lights flared in the drive and the truck came to a halt.

Ron was as white as Wonderbread, without a speck of native blood, but it hadn't stopped him from loving his Maggie. The cowboy and the Indian, he'd called them.

His humor was one of the things Maggie so admired. She called him a truly joyful man. Michaela's throat tightened as she thought of that. He wasn't joyful now that she had gone.

Gone…

How long *had* she been gone? She remembered his note asking her to call him and guilt flared inside her.

He must be worried sick.

She could just make him out as he crushed out the glowing orange tip of his cigarette and glanced anxiously at the house.

Then he hurried toward the house, triggering the security light, which popped on, illuminating him in the drive. He wore his habitual attire of worn cowboy boots and loose jeans held low on his narrow hips by a belt with a brass buckle shaped like a moose. His T-shirts all looked the same, with a pocket over his left breast to hold his cigarettes.

Today his shirt was forest-green, stretching over his potbelly and covered by a quilted flannel shirt. Her gaze flicked back to the new pair of dungarees. She frowned. Only one reason for him to buy new jeans when the old ones were still fit to wear.

Her gaze turned critical. He was thinner and his worn, tanned face seemed to droop. He walked as if his bones ached. He wore his grief like a new coat that did not suit him. Her aunt's death had hit him hard, too, taking his engaging smile along with it. She wondered if he would ever feel the same again.

Michaela tugged at the kitchen door, surprised to find it locked. She flipped back the dead bolt and stepped out on the porch.

"Ron! I'm okay. Sorry if I worried you."

She took a step out onto the wet lawn to meet him.

Ron trudged forward, huffing as he did now from the slightest exertion.

A wisp of white mist swept down from above like a squall of blowing snow, gathering into the familiar features of her aunt Maggie. She waved her hands, as if trying to stop a bus. What was she doing?

"No," she cried. "It's not him."

"What?" asked Michaela, who, distracted by her aunt's frantic gesticulations, missed Ron's advance.

Her confused expression froze on her face as he hauled back and slapped her with all his might. She staggered and fell. The skin at her knees tore at the impact with the ground. Her cheek burned and her ear made a whistling sound, like air escaping from a pinprick in a balloon. She lifted her hand in dumb amazement, touching the side of her head, coming away with sticky, warm blood dribbling between her fingers. The side of her face throbbed in agony at the blow.

Maggie swept forward to protect her, passing right through Ron.

Michaela couldn't have been more shocked at the attack. Was he so furious with her that he would strike her?

Her mouth gaped as she stared up at him.

"Ron?"

Evil yellow eyes stared down in malevolent triumph.

Nagi.

Chapter 26

Lock the doors and windows, Bess had said. But Michaela had let him in. No, worse—she had come out to meet him, as trusting as a lamb at Easter.

Now she stared up at Ron with different eyes, assessing his strengths and searching for weaknesses. He had heart disease and weak lungs from the smoking. He was shorter than she was, but strong from working on cars in his shop. She should run.

Michaela swung her leg around and tripped him. He fell back to the lawn as she scrambled to her feet, trying to reach the house, but he grabbed her by the hair and yanked.

Ron's voice, but not Ron's voice, spoke to her. "I have you now."

She lost her footing as he dragged her down the steps.

She kicked uselessly, pounding her fists against his fingers knotted in her hair. Maggie screamed and swooped away, flying toward the woods.

Ron threw her down the stairs and lifted a leg to stomp on her face, but she rolled away and his boot heel gouged deep into the soft earth.

The sky was lighter now, with pink bands of light streaking across the heavens.

Dawn.

She turned her head toward the tree line and saw him. Sebastian, in his bear form, charged toward them with Maggie.

Ron saw him, too, and had time only to scream before Sebastian threw him down, pinning him between strong front legs. Ron struck the ground hard and his eyes rolled back in his head as he lost consciousness.

Nagi left Ron's body, billowing before them.

Sebastian lifted a mighty front paw to strike Ron, but Michaela screamed at him.

"Stop! Nagi has left him."

The bear moved off the motionless man as Maggie swept forward to hover beside Ron.

Sebastian ran to Michaela. She did not cower as he lifted onto his hind legs and grabbed her in his huge arms, pulling her away from Ron's fallen body.

"Did you kill him?" she asked, staring at her friend.

Sebastian released her, studying her carefully. His eyes narrowed as he saw the blood on her face, and he growled menacingly and stepped between her and Ron.

She turned to find Nagi but was unable to locate him.

Ron had dragged himself to his feet and stood at the

window of his pickup, his eyes fluttering and still rolled so she could see only the whites of his eyes.

"Ron," she called, but he did not heed. He reached behind his seat and grabbed the rifle he used to hunt moose. Then he whirled and fired.

"No!" screamed Michaela as two rounds hit Sebastian.

He reeled but did not fall, staggering backward as Michaela ran toward Ron.

"No! Stop. You'll kill him."

Nothing mattered in this world but saving Sebastian.

She reached Ron, wrapping her fingers around the barrel of the rifle. But Ron jerked it free and lifted the stock to his shoulder, taking careful aim at Sebastian, and fired.

She swung both hands together at Ron's round belly. The impact caused him to fold and she wrenched the gun from his hands.

She stood motionless for one instant, still gripping the barrel, as the swooping sensation caused her to sway. Without ever experiencing this before, she knew intuitively what was happening. She closed her eyes as her body quivered from the vibration of her soul locking back into place.

The disjointed sensation she had carried since her coma was gone. She inhaled sharply at the rightness of this feeling. She felt aware, powerful and whole.

She had done it—her mind, body and soul all moving as one to save her love.

Ron reached for the gun, eyes gleaming yellow and fluttering madly. "You haven't escaped me!"

Sebastian, bleeding from two bullet wounds in his chest, dropped to all fours and charged. Ron lifted a hand to his chest and dropped to his knees before Sebastian reached him.

"No," he howled as his heart stopped its rhythmic beat and Nagi slipped away again. Maggie appeared at Ron's side, trying to embrace him, but her arms slid through his body.

Nagi leaped away once more, howling like a soul in torment.

Sebastian transformed, lifting his arms to the heavens. Above him the wind began to blow as dark, menacing clouds swept in from the west.

"I'll find another body," howled Nagi.

Sebastian clutched Michaela in his arms as he braced for the whirlwind.

"No! If you take her, she will disappear. Stop! I'll give you anything."

Sebastian stared at Michaela. "You did it?"

She nodded. "I'm whole."

Nagi swirled and frothed. "Don't!"

"Stay there and the Thunderbirds will blow you to the four winds."

They came, charging forth on dark swirling clouds, lifting them as Nagi frothed in fury.

Michaela laughed at the cold wind that bore them up into the heavens, carrying them safely away. They landed beside a dry riverbed.

She glanced at the unfamiliar surroundings. They had escaped.

Her elation vanished as Sebastian's legs gave way.

She clutched at him, staring at the holes in his white T-shirt and the dark blood oozing from the openings.

"We need help. Take us to a hospital."

Sebastian pointed to her ear. "You're bleeding."

Michaela glanced helplessly around the dry, rocky ground. There was nothing and no one here. Wilted cottonwood and rock seemed the only available resources.

"What is this place?"

"It was a river when I was a boy. It is near humans, in case…" His voice trailed off.

"Oh, no, you don't. You're not dying on me."

He gave her a weak smile. "All right, rabbit. Make me a circle of stones, a medicine wheel."

She scrambled to re-create the circle he had made for her healing, heaving stones to form a rough ring large enough to accommodate him. When she had finished, he crawled inside.

Please let him live. Two bullets, it was a wonder he hadn't bled to death.

"Fetch my feather."

"Your feather?"

He nodded. "Any feather."

"Can you heal your own wounds?"

"With a feather," he rasped. "Helps me focus."

Michaela scrambled toward the cottonwoods on a scavenger hunt to save Sebastian's life.

She searched in the brush and along the ground but could find no feathers. The seconds ticked to minutes as she continued her frantic search.

Feather, feather, any kind of feather.

Sweat beaded on her forehead as she felt her chance to save Sebastian slipping away. She choked back sobs, refusing to yield to the agony of her failure. Tears dropped to the dry ground as she ran this way and that.

She was in such a state of panic, she nearly did not see him, sitting alone on the large rock beneath the gnarled cottonwood.

But there sat a ghost, still as mist on the water. He watched her with interest as she charged up to him.

"Can you help me? I need a feather."

The ghost startled and then looked behind him, as if certain she spoke to someone else.

"Me?" he asked.

"Yes, you. I need one now, or my friend will die."

"You can see me?"

"Please, not now. Can you help me?"

Still gaping, he rose to his feet. "I saw a magpie's nest back that way. Might be a feather in there."

Michaela ran in the direction he pointed. He beat her there, his vaporous arm extended through the branches and disappeared into the bush.

Michaela pushed back the foliage and found the tightly woven nest lined with downy feathers.

Would such a small feather work? She took the entire empty nest and was just about to go when she saw it, on the ground—a long perfect gray feather from the wing of a magpie. She hoisted it and ran back the way she came.

Sebastian lay motionless in the circle, blood running from his wounds onto the thirsty ground.

She fell to her knees beside him, holding out the nest in one hand and the feather in the other. He opened one eye and looked at her offering. A smile formed.

"You found one."

"Will it work?"

"Yes, rabbit." He gripped the clear, pointed quill of the feather and passed it over his wound.

Sebastian chanted as he worked his healing magic, using the small feather to direct his healing powers. His thick hide and bulk of muscle had taken most of the impact. One bullet had passed through his shoulder, lodging against the blade, narrowly missing his neck. The other was more troublesome, having pierced between two ribs, nicking his left lung and collapsing it. He tasted his blood with each breath and feared if he coughed the frothy pink blood he would frighten Michaela, so he allowed it to collect in his rib cage, flowing into the cavity left by his shrunken lung and frothing from the hole in his torso like soap bubbles.

His breath whistled unnaturally through the ragged hole. If he were an ordinary bear, it would have been a kill shot. But not an immediate kill. He still would have had time to finish the one who had shot him before dying.

But this man was already dead. Nagi had used Ron's body, even after Sebastian had rendered it unconscious.

He closed his eyes and chanted, feeling the bullets draw out of the tunnels of gore they had created. Behind them, the tissue mended, scarred first, then healed.

He tried a breath. The whistle had ceased. He filled his lungs with air and, finding they both worked, he sighed. Good. On the second breath, the bullets emerged, dropping to the ground.

Michaela picked up both flattened pieces of lead, her mouth opened in an astonished little O.

"Now you," he said, motioning to the circle.

"You are okay?"

"Perfectly." He lifted the bloody shirt to show his unblemished skin, still smeared with his blood.

She grimaced at the sight but lay in the circle with her head pointing north.

Sebastian raised his hands to judge her injuries. The scrapes on her knees were minor, but her eardrum was ruptured by the blow. He fanned the soft gray feather over her wounds as he chanted, asking the help of the Spirit of his father as he worked to mend the damage.

As he labored, he stared at her serene face, at the trust and the peace.

Michaela had done it. She was whole once more. Nagi could no longer track her like a wolf after a wounded caribou. But she could see him and all his ghosts. She was a true Niyanoka. In time she would be the threat Nagi feared.

She was no longer his. Once he finished healing these small injuries, she would have no further need of a mangy Inanoka, trailing after her like a lovesick bull elk. The time had come to give her up.

The ceremony complete, he tucked the feather behind her ear. She retrieved it, stowing it carefully inside the back pocket of her slacks.

"You never know," she said.

"I used to tie one in my hair."

"Smart move." She sat up and he helped her to her feet. With the contact came the flow of love and respect she held for him. He broke the contact as soon as he was able.

She stood before him, waiting.

Michaela heard a familiar voice coming from behind her.

"Miss, can you help me? I've lost my horse."

She turned to see the ghost who had located the feather. He looked at them sheepishly from the far side of the medicine wheel.

"What is it?" asked Sebastian, reminding her that he could not see this soul.

"A ghost. He wants me to help him find his horse. He got me the feather."

Sebastian glanced off in slightly the wrong direction. "Then you should help him."

"Find his horse?"

"He's confused. He doesn't know he's dead. You must help him cross onto the Spirit Road."

She faced the ghost. "How am I supposed to do that?"

"Who's dead?" asked the ghost.

Michaela looked at the stooped old specter.

"Sir, we were speaking of you. You're, well, you've passed on. I mean, you haven't passed on, but you aren't alive."

He grew slightly more transparent. "That why nobody will talk to me?"

"That's why. How did you get here?"

"My horse threw me, and when I came to, the boy was gone."

"I think perhaps you were gone—died, that is."

He threw his hat to the ground, then rested his hands on his hips and stared down at it. "Explains a lot." He glanced at Michaela. "Balderdash never threw me before."

"I'm sure he never intended to. You need to look for the Spirit Road and follow it."

"I see it every night. It touches the earth on the northern horizon. But I've been looking for my horse, you see."

"If your horse is alive, you can't help it, and if it's dead, it already went that way."

He smiled, showing an empty hole where his teeth should have been, and then retrieved his hat.

"Tonight, follow the road. Will you?"

"Yes, ma'am." He tipped his cowboy hat and wandered up the bank toward the north. "Maybe I'll find Balderdash that way."

Michaela turned to Sebastian, who stood rubbing his neck as he watched her.

"What?"

"Strange to hear only one side of a conversation. Makes you sound like a Heyoka." He pointed toward his temple.

"I guess I am one."

"What do they look like, the ghosts?"

"Sort of like people made of mist or water. It depends. The bad ones are gray or black, the color of smoke from burning rubber. The murdered one I saw had a red sheen." She gasped, recalling something. "Ron! We can't leave him lying out in the road."

"Nagi might be waiting there for us. He can't track you, but…"

"I know. My father said once I was healed, Nagi could only find me if I crossed his path." She thought a moment. "Can we land nearby and sneak in?"

Sebastian thought for a moment and then nodded his consent. In a few minutes, they were riding on the wings of the Thunderbirds once more. This time, Michaela enjoyed the ride, catching sight of the talons of the bird at one point.

They landed on the southern side of the house, near the road. Sebastian went first, scouting for danger, and she trailed behind, watchful for all he could not see.

"Do you sense him?" he whispered.

"No."

The cabin came in sight. She saw Ron's body, sprawled out on the grass before his truck.

Michaela caught movement from her periphery and tensed. Sebastian stepped before her, his muscles taut and braced to defend. Michaela turned toward the porch and saw the couple descend.

"It's safe," said Maggie. "He's gone. We were waiting. I knew you'd come back."

Michaela laid a hand on Sebastian's arm. "It's all right."

His shoulder relaxed. "What is it?"

"My aunt."

Both ghosts smiled peacefully at her.

"Maggie and Ron. They say it's safe."

Sebastian glanced around, his eyes shifting to glimpse what he could not see.

Ron seemed taller as a ghost. He stood straight and proud, clasping his love's hand.

Michaela felt responsible for his death. "I'm so sorry that he used you that way."

Ron nodded. "Me, too. You know I'd never hurt you, right, pumpkin?"

"I know."

Sebastian shifted uncomfortably.

"My heart gave out. Couldn't take the strain. It's been giving me the devil's time for years."

"I've been waiting for him." Maggie nudged Ron, who moved just like he would have if he still had his body. "He always keeps me waiting."

The two faced each other, touching foreheads. Maggie remembered Michaela first. "You'll be all right now without us, won't you? We won't go if you need us."

"I'll be fine." Michaela was surprised to get the words out without crying. "I'll miss you both."

"Care to see us off?" asked Maggie.

She nodded and spoke to Sebastian. "They want us to see them off."

He frowned.

The ghosts wandered toward the tree line, stepping right beside Ron's body without a glance.

Michaela had to stop. "Ron?"

They paused.

"What about…?" She pointed.

"Oh, that." He frowned at his body as if regarding some nuisance. "Bury it beside Maggie's grave."

"I will."

They were off again and she followed, leading Sebastian along through the line of trees to the stream beyond.

"Far enough," said Maggie.

Michaela gripped Sebastian around the waist.

"I wish I could kiss you goodbye," said Michaela.

"Me, too, sweetheart. We'll see you again. You take good care of those babies. You hear? I know you'll be a terrific mom."

Michaela's gaze shot to Sebastian for his reaction.

Chapter 27

Michaela held her breath as she stared at Sebastian, waiting for his reaction to the news that he was to be a father. It was not until he gave none that she recalled he could not hear Maggie's words. She alone could hear ghosts.

"Thank you," she whispered.

Ron and Maggie clasped both hands and faced each other as if about to join in marriage. Their bodies grew transparent, like air and water.

"Wait," called Michaela.

But they were gone.

She leaned against Sebastian. "I wanted to tell them I love them."

"They know that already," he assured her.

She sniffled a few moments as he stroked her back. Gradually she returned to herself and to him.

Michaela lifted her tearstained face to him, her mouth open in astonishment.

"Look where we are."

He glanced down at the blueberry patch.

She lifted her hands to his shoulders and pressed her damp face to his chest. "This is where we first met."

"And now you're whole again," he said, trying to stand straight, like the man he would never be.

"Thanks to you." When he did not return her smile, her own faded.

He grasped her chin. "No, little rabbit. It is your power that renders him blind. Not mine. You don't need me anymore."

Her eyes widened as the implication of his words struck her.

"I *do* need you," she insisted.

He tried for a reassuring smile and failed. "It's time for you to seek your own people, go to your father's family in Montana and begin your training with your father."

"No! I want to stay with you."

"But you cannot live in my world and I am not welcome in yours."

"You don't love me?" Her pitiful voice nearly made him weep.

"It does not matter."

"It is all that matters."

Should he tell her the truth—that he had loved her since the day he first picked her up and could not put her down? No, this would make their parting more difficult.

"What can I say to make you believe me? I love you with all my heart, Sebastian."

She reached for him and he stepped back. Her hands fell to her sides.

"Don't leave me over something I can't control. I didn't choose to be Niyanoka. I won't be if it means losing you."

"We cannot change what we are."

"But we can choose who we love."

"It's not love, rabbit. It is need you feel, that's all. But you don't need me anymore."

"Stay," she begged.

"So you can outgrow me?" He shook his head. "No."

Her expression turned fierce. "This isn't about me, is it? It doesn't matter how much I love you, because you're not good enough. You're ready to throw me away because you're too stubborn to accept that you might deserve to be loved."

He stared at her in speechless astonishment. No one had ever spoken to him like this. His scowl deepened as he recognized that she was right. He didn't deserve her. He'd thought so from the start.

"Animals only believe their senses. That right?" Her posture and her glower challenged him.

"That is so," he said, feeling his conviction shaken by the thunderclap she laid on him.

She pulled up her sweater and then grabbed his hand, pressing it to the warm, soft skin of her belly. Her voice held its hard edge. "Well, then, chew on this—I'm pregnant."

His world tilted as this lightning strike rocked him. "What?"

"I'm carrying your babies."

He stared at her upturned face. "It's not possible."

"Because only a woman who loves you can bear your child?"

He nodded.

She pressed harder on his hand. "Well, I'm carrying twins."

He closed his eyes and knew it was so. Felt it in her thoughts, emotions. Her father had told her this in her dreams.

Sebastian's grip slackened, and he swayed at the internal wind that ripped through him, sweeping away all his beliefs in an instant.

"Could it be so?" He dared to hope.

"Ask Bess. She sees them, I'm sure of it, or their auras."

"But Niyanoka and Inanoka cannot couple. We are different species."

"Well, somebody got that wrong, too."

The truth she had been telling him showered down on him like warm rain. He clasped her to him, sending the air from her lungs. He loosened his grip and rocked her gently. Joy, pure and sweet, bubbled within him, but it tempered when he felt her uncertainty. He drew back to look into her upturned anxious face.

"Sebastian, I need to know how you feel about me." She stiffened and braced herself with her chin high, as if waiting for a blow.

He kissed her, once, twice and then a third time, until she was breathless.

"Little rabbit, you have my heart as long as it is beating."

She shook her head. “Not good enough. I want you here and in the Spirit World.”

He pulled her close. “Then we will walk that trail together.”

“Yes,” she sighed. “Together.”

He drew back as another worry jabbed at him. “What will our children be, Skinwalkers or Children of the Spirit?”

“Does it matter? We’ll love them, whatever they are.”

He drew her into his arms for another kiss, thinking the world was suddenly sweeter than ever in his memory. She lifted her hands to his shoulders and pressed her damp face to his chest.

She hugged him, sending a warm wave of happiness radiating through him. How could he be so lucky, to win the heart of such a woman?

He held her in his arms, closing his eyes against the unfamiliar burning. His breathing came in a ragged gasp, as if some unseen force closed his windpipe.

Michaela drew back to look up at him.

“Sebastian, are you crying?”

He lifted a hand to his eye and it came back wet. “I never have before.”

“Why now?”

“I can’t believe my fortune. I never dreamed to find a woman who would love a great beast like me.”

She hugged him fiercely, then drew back to give him a smile full of all the promises she had made him, and he knew she would keep every one.

“I never expected to find a man I could trust. But I do, with all my heart.”

He glanced at the low bushes sprinkled with plump berries. He drew a heavy sigh as new uncertainties buzzed within like bees.

She stood waiting before him, a hopeful expression on her sweet face.

He shifted uneasily, thinking of their future together. "I've never been a father before."

"You'll be great."

Nagi billowed at the core of his world. Far on the horizon, the ghosts streamed by in their endless circle, giving him a pleasant and constant breeze. But the view never changed.

Another Seer in the world and now her trail was lost. He would need good luck to find her again.

He tried to satisfy himself with the knowledge that he was timeless, while she had only a few short centuries on earth. She would die and he would try again.

He straightened.

But what if she had offspring? She might raise a nest of Seers. He needed to kill her now—would have already, if not for that meddlesome Inanoka. Their races had not worked together since before the war. It did not bode well for him.

Halflings. They were so smug in their powers, walking on earth, but privy to the workings of the universe. They were not very powerful, but they did have life and that was something he longed for.

The idea struck him fully formed. He contracted at the genius of it and waited while he searched for flaws. No, it could work and it would be *so* easy. Any female would do.

No—not any. She must be strong, big, powerful. Like a female buffalo. But human, yes, human.

If Niyan could father a Halfling race and the great oaf Tob Tob could sire herds or litters or whatever he called his Halfling horde, then why couldn't he do the same?

Children of Nagi. They would be powerful.

He had gone about this all wrong. Using possession to take the living, using ghosts, it was not the same as actually being alive. More like a simulation than the real deal. You couldn't touch or taste or smell.

But to go into a human female and impregnate her—yes. That was something. His own children would be resilient. They could overcome man, despite the Niyanoka. Those hippie freaks hadn't faced a real threat since the Inanoka attacked them. Excising ghosts, healing injured minds and helping humans regain control of their silly little lives. What a joke.

His offspring would give them a real challenge. How many children could he sire in just one month's time?

He ungulated with delight.

It was good to have a plan.

* * * * *

* * *

'THIS EVENING I'm flying to New York for two weeks,' Jasim imparted with a casualness that made her heart sink like a stone. 'That's why I had you brought here. I own this apartment and you'll be comfortable here while I'm abroad.'

'I can afford my own accommodation although I may not need it for long. I'll have another job by the time you get back—'

Jasim released a slightly harsh laugh. 'There's no need for you to look for another position. How would I ever see you? Don't you understand what I'm offering you?'

Elinor stood very still. 'No, I must be incredibly thick because I haven't quite worked out yet what you're offering me….'

His charismatic smile slashed his lean dark visage. 'Naturally, I want to take care of you….'

'No, thanks.' Elinor forced a smile and mentally willed him not to demean her with some sordid proposition. 'The only man who will ever take *care* of me with my agreement will be my husband. I'm willing to wait for you to come back but I'm not willing to be kept by you. I'm a very independent woman and what I give, I give freely.'

Jasim frowned. 'You make it all sound so serious.'

'What happened between us last night left pure chaos in its wake. Right now, I don't know whether I'm on my head or my heels. I'll stay for a while because I have nowhere else to go in the short term. So maybe it's good that you'll be away for a while.'

Jasim pulled out his wallet to extract a card. 'My private number,' he told her, presenting her with it as though it was a precious gift, which indeed it was. Many women would have done just about anything to gain access to that direct hotline to him, but his staff guarded his privacy with scrupulous care.

Before he could close the wallet, his blood ran cold in his veins. How could he have made such a serious oversight? What if he had got her pregnant? He knew that an unplanned pregnancy would engulf his life like an avalanche, crush his freedom and suffocate him. He barely stilled a shudder at the threat of such an outcome and thought how ironic it was that what his older brother had longed and prayed for to secure the line to the throne should strike Jasim as an absolute disaster....

* * *

What will proud Prince Jasim do if Elinor is expecting his royal baby? Perhaps an arranged marriage is the only solution! But will Elinor agree? Find out in DESERT PRINCE, BRIDE OF INNOCENCE by Lynne Graham [#2884], available from Harlequin Presents® in January 2010.

HPEX0110B

Silhouette®

nocturne™

COMING NEXT MONTH

Available December 29, 2009

#79 LAST OF THE RAVENS • Linda Winstead Jones
Bren Korbinian suspects that his lineage will end with him—as the last of his kind, a raven shape-shifter, there is only one woman in the world who is meant for him. Never expecting to find her, he's stunned when Miranda Lynch visits his mountain and awakens his desire. But there are those determined to make sure that Bren is the last…even if it means eliminating them both.

#80 SENTINELS: WOLF HUNT • Doranna Durgin
Born as a wolf and forced into human shape by the evil Atrum Core, Jet has only one mission: take down Sentinel Nick Carter. To save her pack and gain her freedom, she'll need to destroy the shape-shifting timber wolf. Which, after discovering their animal attraction, is easier said than done….

SNCNMBPA1209